Rosebud, With Fangs

Rosebud, With Fangs

Beverly Keller

A Harper Trophy Book
Harper & Row, Publishers

To Barbara Lalicki

Rosebud, With Fangs

One

If my mother hadn't been desperate, we would not have found ourselves in that wilderness. We would never have confronted EVIL or the beast, the beast that, I have reason to suspect, may linger with us even now.

Still, I suppose any parent with four children and no work is likely to get desperate.

Mother lost her job when the auto plant closed. For three months after her unemployment ran out she searched for work, until she had trouble buying even beans and potatoes.

Then she got the letter.

"I never met my great-uncle Elmo." She looked more stricken than happy—I suppose good news can be a shock to someone who hasn't known much of it. "Imagine. I'm his only <u>heir</u>. Fifty acres, with a house on it!"

9

"And hardly any money," Emmaline murmured.

Emmaline is thirteen, a year older than I. To look at her, you'd never dream she grew up in the housing projects. With her long, fine black hair, her pale, perfect skin, her wide, heavy-lashed green eyes, Emmaline looks like some romantic heroine temporarily down on her luck. With the time she spends in front of the mirror, she ought to look like the best of Snow White, Cleopatra, and Helen of Troy. Emmaline reads romantic novels, and poetry, and every self-improvement article in the magazines people throw in the trash for blocks around. Then she cuts out all the sweepstakes entries that haven't expired, especially the ones that offer luxury sedans or Caribbean vacations. Mama complains about the stamps Em uses, so Em has to agonize over which entries to mail.

My sister Oralee, now, looks as if she were *born* down on her luck. At seven, Oralee is already too far gone for any self-improvement program. Her knees and elbows stick out like burls on her spindly legs and arms. Her limp, pale, sparse hair won't hold a braid or a curl or a bow. The minute she puts on her shoes, the backs of her socks slide down into them. Oralee's eyebrows and lashes are almost white. Her eyes are a pale blue, set in a squint that even eyeglasses don't improve, and the skin under her nose seems permanently chapped. Even hand-me-downs look tackier on Oralee than they would on anybody else.

What hurt so much later was remembering that my brother Harry, before the wilderness, was a beautiful little boy. *Rosebud,* Mama called him when he was a baby, I think because of the high color in his cheeks and the soft dewy sheen to his skin. Even at five, his dark brown hair got damp around his forehead when he slept.

Mama signed the papers the lawyers sent, then sat down and figured what our inheritance really amounted to. "After the lawyers' share, Elmo's money will get us off welfare for maybe six months, if we stay here. Then, if there's still no work to be had, it's back on welfare with the money gone, and nothing any better than it was. That fifty acres is our only real hope for a change."

"But it's in the wilderness!" Emmaline protested.

Mama looked out the window with the plastic over the broken bottom pane, out at the street with the trash blowing around, out at the jobless men who looked as aimless, as used-up and unwanted, as the trash. "Baby, what do you think this is?"

Emmaline was close to crying. "You can't take us someplace a hundred miles from nowhere!"

"Not quite a hundred." Mama spread out one of

11

the maps the lawyers had sent, a big AAA road map. "There's a little town right off the two-lane blacktop. See that dot? Then it's about fifty miles—"

"To where there's no road at all," I said.

"Don't you start, Agnes." Mama spread a county map over the AAA map. "It's about fifty miles to a gravel road, which, after about thirty miles, turns into"—over the county map, she spread a hand-drawn map—"a dirt road, which, after another thirty miles becomes a kind of "—she unfolded a surveyor's map and peered at it—"trail, which leads to our place."

Emmaline groaned, then went on filling out sweepstakes entries, and cutting out proof-of-purchase seals to go with them. Oralee had spent hours scouring the neighborhood trash for boxes and wrappers that had the proof-of-purchase seals Em needed.

"We have to look at it, at least," Mama insisted. "There's a creek a few yards from the house, and hundreds of miles of forest around it. Listen, this might be a paradise. Some rich person might buy it from us—just snap it up for a vacation hideaway. Maybe one of those survival groups would buy it for a retreat. If Elmo was such a recluse, he might even have been a miser. There could be a fortune buried on the property."

"Wow!" Setting Forbisher on the table, Harry

leaned over the maps. Harry leaned so far that the chair he was kneeling on slipped out from under him.

As he fell, he put out his arms so his chin wouldn't hit the table edge. The heel of his right hand slid on Em's papers and as he hit the floor on his back, all the entry forms and little seals Em had filled out and cut out and matched fluttered down on him.

"Maybe a survival group would buy *him,*" Emmaline growled as Mama hauled Harry up and checked him for damage. "If they could cope with him, they'd know they were prepared for the end of civilization."

It was true that Harry had a phenomenal talent, amounting to genius, for attracting trouble. He was bright and sweet and eager to be helpful, with no meanness in him. Harry was just a natural catastrophe.

Satisfied that my brother was only bruised, Mama began folding the maps. "Look, what do we have now? An old car not worth fixing, a few sticks of furniture, a television, our clothes. . . . Harry, what has Forbisher been in?"

Forbisher had plainly been in something gooey, something that caused his mangy hair to stick to the maps. He was a battered derelict of a bear, with eyes that didn't match, an off-center nose, one

13

drooping ear, a limp, lumpy body, and a tendency to shed. He'd belonged to Emmaline until she outgrew him, then to me, then Oralee, and finally Harry.

Over the years, Forbisher had lost a lot—an ear, part of his nose, one eye, some stuffing, and an amazing amount of hair. Mama repaired him with whatever she could scrounge, but there was no way she could make him like new.

Harry cherished him. Nobody in the family, not even Emmaline, had the heart to tell my brother he was too old for a teddy bear. Forbisher was, after all, the only being in this world that never disapproved of Harry.

In the next weeks, Mama sold the car and the furniture and even the television set.

Then she bought a motor home. "A motor hovel," Emmaline called it. It was an ancient van from the sixties, the kind you see in old movies about hippies. The metallic orange body was decorated with fluorescent pink and green and purple flowers and arabesques. "I would die being seen in this thing!"

Mama was calm. "Nobody will know us where we're going. With new plugs and points and battery, and the brakes relined, it'll get us there, which is all it has to do."

Inside the van were a toilet, a sink, and a two-burner stove, none of which worked. Mother paid an out-of-work neighbor twenty dollars to fix them. There was a table, covered with chipped yellow Formica, and two benches that could be made into beds.

We used our blankets and sheets to reupholster the benches and curtain off the toilet. Then we scrubbed out the van. This was enough to kill any interest in camping for the rest of my life.

Mama stocked the van with five-gallon cans of water, an extra fan belt and radiator hoses, a fluorescent lantern, rice, beans, lentils, split peas, powdered milk, and peanut butter. She even spent seven dollars on an activity book and marking pens for my brother Harry.

This was not a foolish extravagance. Anything that kept Harry occupied and out of trouble was a brilliant investment.

So we set out for our new life, and the wilderness.

I was homesick minutes after we pulled away from the housing project. But, like Mama, I realized things weren't going to improve for us if we stayed where we were. When you live in a depressed neighborhood of a big city in hard times, you expect life will be better almost anywhere else.

I was scared, but Emmaline complained so long

and so hard, I had to talk brave. That, or boot her out of the van.

"Hey," I said, "remember when we used to go to school with our lunch money hidden in our shoes in case we got mugged? Those were the good old days, when we had lunch money. Remember when we looked forward to school just because of the lunch program? Those lunches weren't so great, either, but they beat the give-away cheese and marked-down bread we had at home."

I sounded to myself like some stand-up TV comic, and I'm not sure I made Mama feel any better, but Em was quiet for a time.

I'm a pretty good talker, at least with my family. It's probably because I read so much. I started reading before I started school. Being even more nearsighted than Oralee, I loved books because the print was something I could see clearly without glasses. Even today my idea of paradise is to be locked up in a library—preferably a library with a bakery attached.

Reading, you pick up a lot of information. You also pick up a way of talking and even thinking that makes you feel alien, sometimes, around people your age. So you tend to read more, and daydream more, and fit in less.

I am also very sensible and down-to-earth—so

sensible I remind myself of a forty-year-old banker at times.

The drive west was one I'll remember all my life.

Sleeping on a van bed padded with old sheets and blankets was merely miserable. The torture was spending those days and nights in close quarters with Harry. He never tried to make trouble. He didn't tease, or sulk, or even ask for much. Of course, he lost the caps of his marking pens right away, but he didn't make a fuss when the ink dried out.

Harry never tried to be a pest. It was just that he was still in the first stages of being in love with the world. Every time we passed a dog, any dog, Harry cried, "Oh, wow! A bloodhound!" or "Look! Look! A real sheepdog!" Every crow he announced as an eagle. At every sleek new sedan, it was "Hey! I bet that's a Secret Service car!"

It is not easy to put up with good cheer and enthusiasm all day long, especially not when you're trapped in a van.

Whenever we stopped, Harry collected rocks. He presented each rock for our inspection. "See? See those shiny specks in it? I bet that's gold. Pure gold. Probably worth a fortune." He showed everything to Em first.

"There must be some way," she said grimly, "to teach him to sulk."

On the fourth day we ran out of clean clothes, so we turned off at a small town. Emmaline and I went to the Laundromat while Mama took Harry and Oralee to a market for bread and apples and a couple of new pens for him.

Em or I should have turned out the pockets of Harry's clothes, but we were tired and stiff and hot. She threw our laundry into a machine and I dumped in detergent. Even when we heard the noise, like a gang rumble in a rock quarry, we didn't realize at first what it was.

Anybody who grows up in housing projects just naturally expects to be blamed for anything that goes wrong. We stopped the machine and fished out our dripping wash and ran for the door, before anybody could call the manager.

I felt like a low, disgusting specimen, but Em said, "Agnes, we'll never convince anybody that kids who ride around in a hippie van didn't put rocks in the machine on purpose." She dropped the wet clothes in the van sink. "As soon as we get out of town, we'll write the Laundromat and promise to send five dollars a month until the damage is paid."

"Where will we get five dollars a month?"

"After these days on the road with Harry, we've *earned* an allowance."

"I mean, where would we get it?"

"Pray Uncle Elmo was a miser."

Mother didn't even ask about the soggy clothes in the sink. She was that undone, and eager to get out of town.

In the market, Harry had backed into a soft drink display, sending bottles rolling all over the floor. Coming out of the store, he'd walked into an empty shopping cart, which careered across the parking lot, hit a parked Harley-Davidson motorcycle, and ricocheted off to roll across the main street. Motorists trying to avoid the cart caused a train of skids and dented bumpers and a very hostile traffic policeman.

Three hours and more than a hundred miles later we stopped for lunch, and Mama noticed the clothes in the sink.

Harry gave up rocks. Instead, he collected leaves every time we stopped, and piled them in the corners of the benches.

Not only do leaves get dry and crumbly after a few days, they sift into the bedding, and they harbor an incredible number and variety of tiny, tiny bugs. These tiny, tiny bugs took only a short time to turn into loathsome insects and small, sinister worms, all determined to make their homes in sheets and pajamas.

After that, Em put Harry's new pens before him every morning after breakfast and ordered him to do nothing but draw.

By the sixth day, the six-lane highway had given

19

way to four lanes, then to a two-lane blacktop road. The landscape, as far as we could see, was flat, brown, and desolate, punctuated by dead brush and tumbleweeds and a few ruined fences. Every twenty or thirty miles we'd pass a two-pump gas station attached to a whitewashed shack with dirty windows and a sign that said EATS, or a moldering, abandoned Giant Orange stand.

Mama stopped a couple of times to check the maps, then passed them back to Harry to fold. Most of the time Oralee slept, stunned by the monotony, I think. Emmaline and I gazed out at the flat land, wondering if our inheritance would look like this.

At least Harry was quiet, busy with his pens. They were cheap stick pens, a red and a blue, but he seemed content with them.

After a while, the two lanes gave way to one, and the asphalt to gravel, and the gas pumps were more decrepit and farther spaced, with no cafés attached.

By mid-afternoon, Mama said, "This can't be right. Hand me up those maps, Harry."

She pulled over to the side, which wasn't really dangerous. We hadn't met another vehicle for hours, and we could see the road for miles in either direction.

Mama spread out the road map. "That's odd. We

were supposed to pass a little town miles back. See that dot? And that dot was off a two-lane blacktop."

We drove another mile on the gravel road, with the gas gauge getting closer to E.

Mama pulled over again and looked closer at the map. "It just makes no . . . *Harry!*"

My little brother had finished his activity book hours earlier, but he hadn't complained, or bothered anybody. He had just sat quietly on the bench behind Mama, connecting the dots on the road map with his red and blue pens. He'd worked so carefully, we all had to squint at the maps to figure out which were the roads and which were Harry's connect-the-dots lines.

"I can't even be sure where we got off the right road," Mama said at last. "The one we've been following doesn't seem to be on any of the maps. I'd hate to be stalled out here miles from nowhere."

"I say we give Harry an empty water can and send him for gas." Em's voice was low and hard.

"Don't be silly," Mama snapped.

"Besides," I added, "we haven't passed a gas station for hours."

"Good." Em said. "With any luck, we'll never see him again."

"That's enough of that," Mother told her. "We'll just have to hope there's a station somewhere up ahead. Then we can worry about getting back on the right road."

We drove on for miles, between barren brown hills, until I saw a dusty track meandering off to our right. Before I could speak, Mama said, "We'll have to chance it. It may lead to a farmhouse."

We turned right and rocked along the dirt road, blinded by the dust, for another five or six miles. Then the road began to ease gently downhill, and there in a hollow ahead was a tiny town. We could see all of it, two blocks long and a block wide, with a grassy town square in the center.

On the corner of the first street we came to was a single-pump gas station. It was clean, and neat, and deserted.

We drove down the street, past a feed store and a repair shop, both abandoned, like the café and social club across from them.

The next street bordered the square. On our right was a bank, then a grocery, then a pharmacy. On the short street facing us, at the far end of the square, was a red brick two-story building flanked by dirt parking lots. Over the building's wooden double doors were gold letters that read CITY HALL.

There were no parking meters, no traffic signs, and no traffic, not a vehicle or a living thing to be seen.

22

We parked outside the grocery, and stepped out of the van into a silence so complete we dared make no sound ourselves.

The grocery store was locked. Through the clear doors we saw it was small, with nobody inside and not much on the shelves.

"I don't understand," Mother said. "Here it is, three o'clock on a weekday afternoon, no holidays in the month, no sign of a parade or a catastrophe, and everything is closed."

A man came out of the city hall and cut across the town square toward us, his footsteps hushed by the grass.

He crossed the street and stopped a few feet from us. He was thin and old, with skin as dry and dead as parchment. His eyes were so pale they seemed to have no color, but they were hard and flat as he stared at us.

"You have a very . . . peaceful town," Mother greeted him.

"Leech," he snapped.

Her face got pink. "I beg your pardon?"

"Raymond Leech."

I could see Mama was embarrassed, but she was so focused on our predicament she didn't pause. "I wonder if you know where we might get gas, Mr. Leech."

"No."

23

"The gas station we just passed seems closed," she persisted.

"Yes."

"If we don't get gas," she went on, "we're stuck here."

Raymond Leech looked at us, taking in our old clothes and worn-out drugstore sneakers. Then he looked at our van.

"Sheriff!" he shouted.

Oralee grabbed my hand. Harry stepped back, and Em put her hand on his shoulder.

Another man hurried out of City Hall, as if he'd been waiting for the summons, and cut across the square. As he strode toward us, I saw he was about fifty, heavyset, with a square ruddy face, a short neck, and eyes as icy and hostile as the older man's.

Raymond Leech jerked his head toward us. "They need gas to get out of town, Sheriff."

The sheriff gazed at us as if trying to connect us with some "Wanted" poster. "Can you make it back to the station?" he asked my mother.

"Just," she said.

From the edge of my eye, I saw a third man unlocking the glass door of the pharmacy. He came out, then locked the door again behind him. Lean and tall, with straight black hair and sun-leathered skin, he wore jeans and cowboy boots, a denim

24

shirt with fold-lines still in it, and sunglasses with mirror lenses that hid his eyes. "Trouble, Marlowe?" he asked the sheriff.

"Just people out of gas," Leech said.

"Give 'em gas to get out of town, Shaw," Marlowe said.

"Just out?" Shaw's voice revealed as little as his mirror-lensed glasses.

"As far as you can get 'em," the sheriff replied.

Harry, who was as full of trust as a kid who's never known a bad day, seemed not at all aware of how unwelcome we were. He kept looking over at the town square, with its soft grass and water fountain and mildewed-looking statute.

"Could we go over to the fountain while—" Oralee began.

"No!" Raymond Leech told her. "This is no place for children."

Mama was flushed with anger, but we were lost, and out of gas, and at the mercy of these strange and surly men. She herded us back into the van and drove to the gas station.

Shaw came striding down the street from where we'd left him, and Mama got out of the van and checked the tires and wiped the windshield, and then reached in and got the maps.

Shaw stood by the pump, facing the flowers and curlicues on our van as the tank was filled.

"Could you tell me how to get back on Road 113?" Mama asked him.

He didn't even turn those mirrored lenses toward her.

She spread the road map against the side of the van so he couldn't ignore it. "Where are we now?"

"Not on the map."

Tossing that map in the window, she spread out another. "Here's where we want to go."

He replaced the nozzle on the pump and put his finger on the map. "You head down the road you came in until you get to the crossroad . . ."

As he went on talking, I gazed out the window. I'd never seen a more forsaken town. It was immaculate, with not so much as a scrap of paper on the pavement, without a stray dog or even a scavenging sparrow. Even more eerie was the silence. The only sounds were the rustle of the map, Mama's murmur, and Shaw's voice.

". . . straight, until you come to a fork. You take this leg." Shaw put his finger on the map. "Be sure you don't take the other. That would lead you into the wilderness. There are . . . things . . . beyond it that you wouldn't want to see. You just take this fork, and keep going. Keep going until you're well away from here."

He took her money and gave her change, and as we drove away he stood quite still, his mirror lenses reflecting our departure.

"I don't know. It's getting so late. Maybe we would have been better staying there for the night," Mama said. "Still, we might as well drive as far as we can while there's light. Em, you stay up here and hold the map. See, we go to this fork, take this road . . ."

With Em sitting up front beside Mama, I stretched out on a bench and dozed, in spite of the rough road and the van's jouncing.

I was wakened by the low sun through the windshield. From the sound of the van's laboring, I could tell we were on an upgrade, and when I sat up I saw that the land was easing into rounder hills. There were a few stunted evergreens on either side of the road, and boulders scattered as if a giant had tossed them around in a careless temper.

As the road climbed, the trees grew thicker. When I opened a window, the outside air was dry, thin, and cool, sharp with the scent of pine needles.

We came to a fork in the dirt road, and Mama asked Em, "Which way did he say?"

Em looked down at the map in her lap and murmured in a drowsy voice, "Left."

The road was a rutted track. As we drove on, the trees were taller, closer together, until there was no way of knowing whether the sun was setting, or the twilight was the perpetual dusk of a great forest. The only sound was the straining and rattling of our van blundering through that enormous, enveloping hush. Before long, the trees were so close to us that their branches scraped the van roof.

"I'd never try this in wet weather, I'll tell you that." Mama steered around the biggest humps and the deepest ruts, as the engine moaned and complained.

The van struggled over what was now barely a track, and the branches scratched the windows as we passed, and then the trail simply ended. The trees stood, impenetrable, like a phalanx of silent warriors massed to repel us.

"Let me see that." Mama reached for the map Em had. "Oh, Em." My mother sounded as close to despair as I'd ever heard her. "Em, you've been holding the map upside down."

I realized then that, between my older sister and my little brother, not even an inheritance could save this family.

TWO

The only way to move was backward. With the branches scraping the windows, Mama couldn't even stick her head out. The van groaned in reverse, and then there was a noise like metal on stone. The engine screamed, but the van didn't move.

We got out into the silent twilight, onto the trail that cut like a gash through the looming forest. I held the flashlight while Mama got down and peered under the van.

"Oh, boy." She stood. "The undercarriage is hung up on a hump."

We tried shoving the van but we couldn't even rock it.

The gloom of the forest was deepening into true dark. The trees seemed like a presence all around us, and the stillness was so deep I felt as if we'd wandered into another planet, or an age earlier than anything we could imagine.

I think Mama felt it. She herded us into the van and opened the battered Styrofoam cooler. "It's too dark to do anything now. We'll eat, and then we can sit around and tell stories."

"No," I said, remembering all the TV movies in which campers sit around in the wilderness and tell ghost stories, only to be killed off, one by one, by something stalking in the night.

We ate. Peanut butter sandwiches, bitter celery, and small hard apples. Then we made up the beds and Mama kept the lantern on and read to us from *Mary Poppins*.

She'd read *Mary Poppins* to Em, and to me, and to Oralee, and taken us all to see the movie. As much as Harry loved to hear Mama read the book, he was thrilled by the movie, squeezing my hand and whispering, "Oh! Oh! Oh!" at the sight of Mary Poppins sailing on the wind, clutching her umbrella and steadying her hat.

Listening to Mama read *Mary Poppins* yet again, I felt almost as I had before I learned that my mother couldn't make the world safe for us. I realized that Mary Poppins, prim and confident, never confused, made the children in her care feel safe, no matter how strange the world around them was.

My mother's not so proper, and not at all immune to confusion or embarrassment or doubt.

On the other hand, who'd want to hug Mary Poppins?

Once Harry and Oralee were asleep, Mama put out the lantern and whispered good night, and I lay wondering if I was the only one in the van awake.

It was the stillness outside that was so unsettling. Night in a housing project is full of voices—people greeting or parting or fighting, babies crying, cats carousing, car doors slamming, late movies on neighbors' televisions.

There were no sounds in this night wood, nothing: not crickets, nor the rush of owl wings, nor even the crack of a twig. I'd seen enough nature films on PBS to know a night forest is supposed to be alive with noises.

Here, the only sounds were the breathing and stirring inside our van.

Now and then I dozed, then woke, listening to the absolute quiet outside.

I lay, not moving, until the darkness bleached to gray, and in the cold near-light, I thought I saw, peering in through the windshield, a face, pale, with the glassy blue stare of a manic doll.

I sat up. "Mama!"

"Agnes?"—my mother's voice—"Are you all right?"

"I thought . . . I thought I saw somebody. . . ."

"You must have dreamed it."

"I guess so." After all, what kind of creature had eyes like a doll's and wandered the wilderness at night peering in windows? "This place sort of . . . gets to you."

"I know." Swinging her feet to the floor, she started putting on her shoes.

"Mama?" It was Em's voice. "Where are you going?"

"You all stay here," Mama said. "Agnes, you lock the door after me."

Now Oralee sat up. "You're not going to leave us?"

"Oralee, you know you and Harry could never walk out of these woods." Mama stood. "And we surely couldn't if we had to carry you."

I kicked off the blanket. "I could come with you. Or Em could."

"Honey, you know how Em's feet blister. And if you came with me, that would mean leaving Oralee and Harry with Em, and you know Em has no patience with Harry. You'll all be safer and I'll worry less if you're here locked in the van."

"But, Mama," Em protested, "what if somebody comes along on the road?"

"Em, who's going to come along on this trail? I doubt if it's been used in years."

Mama stepped out into the chill damp dawn, and I locked the door behind her as she'd told me.

Harry and Oralee stared at me like a couple of cubs dug out of a den, Harry hugging Forbisher tight.

"Okay," I said. "Em and I will make the beds and then we can have breakfast. Oralee, you get the bowls and spoons and milk. Harry, you fill the sugar bowl and get out the cereal."

After we made the beds, we washed in the sink. Four people washing hands and faces in that van involved more jostling and maneuvering and snapping than your average family has in a week.

Then Harry stood on the toilet seat to get a fresh bar of soap off a shelf and somehow his foot slipped.

"He's a total, complete disaster!" Em stormed as I hauled Harry out of the toilet. "If it weren't for him, we wouldn't even *be* here!"

"Come on, Em," I remonstrated. "You're the one who read the map upside down."

She was sensitive about that, so we spent ten minutes yelling before we settled down to breakfast. Even then, Em made Harry sit in the open doorway of the van with his feet outside, though Mama had told us to keep the door locked.

"I refuse to sit down to a meal with any five-year-old who doesn't know better than to fall into a toilet!" my sister fumed.

Harry was already pale and teary, so I didn't make an issue of it. Still, it's sad to see a five-year-old sitting on the floor of an old hippie van with his feet outside. It's even sadder when the five-year-old is cuddling a moth-eaten relic of a teddy bear and eating generic corn flakes with watered milk.

Em ladled sugar on her cereal, both to cover the taste and to avoid looking at Harry, I suspect. Passing me the sugar bowl, she began to eat.

"Aaaaugh!" She scrambled to the sink, groping for a glass.

"Harry, you monster! You beast!" she yelled when she'd downed a glass of water. "You filled the sugar bowl with salt, you toad!"

"Why, Harry? Why?" I demanded.

His tears were spilling over, now. "Both the bags were white, Aggie, and the stuff in them was white, and—"

Em lunged for him. I got her by the arm and Oralee grabbed her around the leg.

"Let me go!" Em yelled. "I'll—"

Snatching up Forbisher, Harry leaped out of the van.

"You'd better run, you little monster," Em yelled. "When I get my hands on you . . ." She pulled away from me and scrambled over Oralee and got to the door before I tackled her.

It was like a TV tag-team match gone bad, me

hanging on to Em, Oralee wrapping her arms around our legs and wailing, "Don't! Don't!"

Wrestling Em away from the door, I struggled over Oralee and jumped out.

"Harry!" I yelled. "It's okay! Harry?"

There was no sign of my brother.

"Harry?" I called.

Oralee climbed out of the van and grabbed my hand.

Em leaped out. "Harry! You get right back here!"

"That's good," I told her. "That's great. That's the way to reassure him."

Facing that woods in the cold morning, with no hint of where my brother was, the three of us moved closer together. Em's rage was fast dissolving into uneasiness.

"Harry!" I yelled. "It's all right!"

It was as if he had never existed. If he'd plunged into that congregation of trees, he'd left no sign. We circled the van, keeping so close we brushed it, shouting for him. When we came back to the open door, we stopped.

"If he's gone any distance," Em said grimly, "you can count on him getting lost."

I called a few more times, my voice swallowed instantly by the silence. The three of us stood for a minute by the van.

"We'd better go after him." Em's voice was subdued.

"I know." Still, I hesitated, as if I could wish Harry back with us.

"We'll leave a note for Mama," Em said. "Come on."

We stepped back into the van. Em scrawled a note on the inside cover of Harry's activity book and propped the book on the sink. I picked up the book Mama had been reading to Oralee and Harry. "We can use pages from this to mark our way so we don't get lost."

"*Mary Poppins*?" Oralee gasped.

"Would you have the heart to tear up Harry's activity book?" I demanded. "Would you dare tear up one of Em's books?"

So we edged into the woods, Em and I trying to navigate with Oralee hanging on to us. Every few feet I stuck a page from *Mary Poppins* on a twig or a bush.

"We have never sunk so low," Em grumbled. "Not only defacing the wilderness, but destroying *Mary Poppins*. Harry!" she called. "Harry, you monster, where are you?"

"Em, don't *do* that!" I said.

"I can't help it. He is a monster. He's a beast. His whole life, he's been driving everybody crazy. He could drive the world crazy! He's a nightmare, a catastrophe!"

"Wonderful." The voice was deep, and very close.

I turned, suppressing a yelp.

The man must have been following us for some time. He seemed not at all surprised to see three girls in ratty old pajamas wandering through a forest. He was fairly tall, forty or fifty years old, with pale smooth skin and blue eyes as clear and cold as a doll's. In that wilderness he wore a gray three-piece suit, and he had no hair, no hair on his head, no eyelashes, no eyebrows. He smiled. His teeth were small and white and even, like a doll's, except for his upper canines, which were slightly pointed.

In a deep wood, there is nowhere to run. And to run would be to invite pursuit.

"This monster—would you be interested in selling it?"

Like my sisters, I was too startled to speak. I couldn't identify his accent.

"Maybe a trade?" he persisted.

"Sell my brother?" Oralee quavered.

The man looked surprised. "Brother?"

I knew better than to talk to strangers, especially strangers in a forest, but the most important thing was to find Harry. "A little boy about five years old with dark hair . . ."

"But you were speaking of a beast, a monster, a catastrophe who could drive whole planets crazy," the man said.

"That's . . . our brother," Em confessed. Then, as if she had to rid herself of all her guilt, she blurted out a catalog of the worst Harry had done, ending with the Laundromat, the market cart, the salt in the sugar bowl. Of course, no thirteen-year-old who reads *The Poems of Percy Bysshe Shelley* is going to tell a stranger about her brother stepping into the toilet.

I was appalled to hear her talking so much, as if she couldn't help herself. Then I glanced at the man, and I felt that even the three of us being there, barefoot, in the woods was not as bizarre as his reaction. As Em went on recounting all the chaos Harry had created, this man stared at her, his china blue eyes wide and unblinking. Unblinking, but far from unliving, for the man was rapt, fascinated by her or her words. "All that talent, that genius, disguised as a five-year-old boy, and you *misplaced* him? He must be found!" The man's voice was urgent. "If you locate him first, meet me back here."

"Why?" Oralee asked.

He looked down at her. He smiled. Those cold blue eyes made me shiver. "So I will know . . . where he is. Where he is . . . safe."

Em punched my arm.

"Well. We'd better keep . . . looking," I muttered, and we inched away from him.

38

Once out of his sight, we scurried away through the trees as fast as we could.

"That man," Em whispered, "is weird!"

I heard him, behind us, call, "Little boy! Come out, little boy!"

"Em." I tried to keep my voice calm. "We've got to find Harry, and we've got to get back to the van."

As she opened her mouth, I said, "Without making any noise. We don't want to draw that man back to us."

"What if he gets Mama?" Oralee whispered.

"Don't be silly," Em hissed, but she and I glanced at each other.

We made our way through the forest as quietly as we could. Then I saw a page on the end of a branch.

Em peered at it. "Page five," she groaned. "We're all turned around!"

"Little boy! Where are you?" The man's voice seemed to be receding.

"Agnes," Em said, "if Mama came back, alone or with help, she's not just going to sit in the van waiting. She'll start looking for us. Somebody has to go back to the van."

"And what?" I asked.

"And get us organized."

It was an interesting choice—to stay in a forest

where a weird man roamed, or to go tell my mother how we'd lost her youngest child.

Still, I wasn't the one who'd chased Harry away.

"I'll go back," I decided.

"No," Em said. "Wait. Maybe Harry's gotten back to the van, or Mama has, or both of them. You don't want to have to come looking for me then. If we split up and she's read our note and is already looking for us, we may never get sorted out. We'd better stay together. We'll go see if they're at the van. If they are, we'll all get out of here somehow. If Harry is, we'll wait together for Mama . . ."

Far off, I heard the man. "Little boy?"

". . . or go look for her together," Em said.

It wasn't easy to find the pages I'd left to mark our search. We took wrong turns, we backtracked, and as we came across one page after the other, I realized how long we'd been away from the van and how far we'd gone. We left each page stuck where it was, hoping we wouldn't encounter it yet again.

Oralee kept stumbling, but not uttering a sound. It would have been easier if she'd sobbed, but she only got more silent each time she stumbled.

Finally, Em carried her.

Em was limping and my legs were aching by the time I saw, through the trees, the fluorescent flowers on our van.

As Em set her down, Oralee ran to the van. "Mama!"

Em and I caught up and got the door open.

The van was empty.

We climbed in, then stood silent like people come home from a family funeral, struck by the strangeness of a once-familiar place. Maybe because our mother wasn't there, Em and I seemed older and steadier than we'd ever known we were.

I shut the door. "First, we've got to decide."

"Decide what?" Em asked.

"Decide . . . what to decide."

Em looked at our sister. "Oralee, do you have to go to the bathroom?"

It was exactly what Mama would have said.

Still, it wasn't easy deciding anything.

"We can't leave Harry out there, Em."

Oralee stood between us, not saying a word.

"Agnes, we have to be here if he comes back. How can we leave word for him to stay put? He can't read."

"We could leave Oralee here."

"Alone? With that man prowling the woods?"

"She can lock the door."

"He could break a window."

Oralee looked from Em to me. Oralee, with her pale eyelashes and squinty eyes and scratched eyeglasses, was the kind of kid who is overlooked even

41

in her own family. Suddenly I pictured Oralee, sniffly and washed-out looking, left alone and terrified.

"If you go wandering after Harry and get lost and Mama doesn't come," Em reasoned, "we've got three of you lost. If she does come, she'll have two of you to look for. If she goes looking alone, she can only look for one of you at a time. If she takes Oralee and me with her, my feet will blister more, and Mama will have to carry Oralee. The only thing you'll do by going out there is make everything worse for everybody."

I wanted to agree with her—except I kept imagining Harry alone with Forbisher, somewhere in that forest.

Em sensed what was on my mind. "We have to eat, Agnes. You can't think right on an empty stomach." She looked at the quartz watch we'd gotten as a premium with gas days before. "It's way past noon. You'll never find him if you collapse from hunger."

"What I'll do is just go a little way into the woods in case he's nearby."

I started at the other end of the van from the place we'd headed into the trees the first time. Sticking more pages from *Mary Poppins* on twigs, I remembered again how Harry loved the part in the movie when Mary Poppins came sailing over the treetops. I remembered how he never fussed about wearing rainboots and pajamas and even coats, girls' coats, handed down from Em to me to Oralee to him. Even when he got hand-me-down chicken pox from Oralee, he seemed to take it as natural. He loved that wreck of a hand-me-down teddy bear. . . .

I found myself crying, afraid to make a sound. Then I realized I'd not heard the man in the gray suit for hours.

Nevertheless, one of the bravest things I've ever done was to yell. "Harry!"

I plunged even deeper into the woods, not so much brave as crazy from the fear, until I was dizzy and sick to my stomach.

Tracing my way back to the van, I imagined how I'd walk in and find Harry there with my sisters.

Emmaline let me in. Neither she nor Oralee spoke. Oralee didn't take her eyes off me. Em was careful not to look at me too long. I think she knew that we could only keep our nerve by acting as if we weren't desperate.

She'd cleaned up from breakfast and made cheese sandwiches.

We sat at the table, the three of us silent. Hungry as I'd thought I was, I couldn't swallow. Em got up and mixed the last of the powdered milk with water and put a glass in front of me.

"You can almost believe that if you try hard enough you can erase what happened." She sat down and scratched with her thumbnail at a speck on the Formica.

I still couldn't swallow the bread and cheese, but I drank the milk. Then we sat a few minutes more.

Em stood up. "I guess it's my turn."

I didn't argue.

I locked the door behind her and wrapped the leftover cheese sandwich and sat with Oralee.

Finally, I thought it might help if I read to her. Em had taken the remains of *Mary Poppins*. The only things left to read in the van were road maps and the books Em had brought from home. *Frankenstein*, I knew, was not the thing to read to my little sister, certainly not at a time like this. I skimmed through the first pages of *The Poems of Percy Bysshe Shelley*. "I'll read you 'The Indian Serenade,'" I told Oralee. "You like Indians." And I read,

> "I arise from dreams of thee
> In the first sweet sleep of night.
> When the winds are breathing low,
> And the stars are shining bright . . ."

"Oh, boy," Oralee muttered in disgust.

I put the book down. "Okay. Twenty questions. I'm thinking of something in this van."

"Why don't we just wait?"

Standing in line with my mother for surplus cheese, or at the welfare agency, moving ahead by inches, I used to think that waiting in line was the hardest work in the world.

But waiting, anywhere, when you don't know whether the outcome will break your heart—that costs even more inside.

Oralee sat, barely moving, so quiet it hurt to watch her.

I got up and chopped our last onion and put it in a pot with what split peas were left and most of the water we had. I was uneasy about using our drinking water, but I knew there was no other way to cook split peas.

I didn't turn the stove on. There was no sense wasting fuel when I didn't know how long my sister might be gone.

As it was, she didn't come back until near dark. Oralee went to the door before I heard anything. Em climbed into the van like an old woman boarding a bus. "I looked everywhere. If he heard me call, he'd be scared enough to make up by now."

Sitting on the floor, she took her shoes off very carefully. With her upper lip caught behind her lower teeth, she peeled her socks off like a bandage from a burn. Then she looked at her feet.

"Oh, Em." There was nothing I could do to help. "You'd better keep them covered."

45

"I think you're supposed to leave them open to the air."

While I couldn't remember the right way to treat blisters, it was plain Emmaline would have to stay off her feet.

By the time the soup was done, and we tried to eat, and did the dishes, it was past bedtime by the quartz watch.

Nobody suggested going out in the dark to search. It would have been senseless. We had only one lantern, and it wasn't a searchlight, so whoever took it would have a terrible time just finding the way back to the van. And we had spent the day searching.

In books, you read that time seems to pass slowly when you're in trouble. That's not the way it was for me. We were exhausted, as much by grief and worry as by searching the woods, so I may have slept a lot. When I was awake though, there was just the ache and fear, and time didn't exist.

I knew that as soon as it was light enough to see, I'd have to go out again to look for my brother. I was terrified that I wouldn't find him. I was even more terrified of what I might find. And I was ashamed that I hadn't been brave enough to search for him through the night.

While I put my shoes on, Em fixed me a bowl of cereal, using the last of the milk she'd mixed.

We didn't wake Oralee.

The morning was gray and damp and cold, as silent as the night. If there were birds or beasts or bugs in that forest, they made no sounds.

I wanted to scramble back into the van and huddle with my sisters. Instead I walked into the woods.

Three

I found page after page from the day before. I peered at the ground for any sign that my brother might have passed.

Then I glimpsed it, no more than a flicker moving among the trees. I knew it instantly. Forbisher was, if nothing else, a distinctive wreck of a bear.

"Harry!" I dashed toward that glimpse of mangy fur.

Then, through the trees, a huge hairy thing came hurtling toward me, clutching Forbisher and snuffling.

I whirled and ran, barely feeling the branches clawing my face.

I didn't see the gully in time. Before I could slow down, I slid on a slippery carpet of leaves into the shallow crater.

"Aggie!"

The voice was my brother's. The voice was so piteous I had to glance up, sure the thing I'd seen running to me was only a hallucination.

The beast crouched at the edge of the gully.

I might never have kept my nerve had it not been for the creature's eyes. Those eyes were the soft, worried, gentle brown eyes of some abused spaniel. Those eyes were enough to melt the heart of a hunter. They were Harry's eyes.

"Aggie . . ."

I have never felt such grief, such pity, such horror.

My brother, my five-year-old brother, had been transformed, somehow. "A monster! A beast!" Em had raged. And that he had become.

I should have been grateful to have found him at all, but his appearance was so ghastly I found it hard not to crawl away from him.

His ears were bearlike, small, pointed, and erect. His snout was shaped like a bear's, but his droopy jowls and the lower fangs that curled up over his top jaws gave him something of a bulldog look. His black nose glistened like an oversized beetle on a head that was otherwise covered with short, flat, blue-gray hair.

The rest of his great shambling body, except for the talons on his four paws, was shaggy, his pelt

49

long, blue-gray, and full of tangles, burrs, and pine needles. When he had run on his hind legs, his posture had been that of an ape, or a very Abominable Snowman.

Even now, I feel almost ashamed to report that he was pudgy. That seemed to me, somehow, a particular outrage. Harry had been a slender, agile little boy. You can't even *respect* a pudgy monster.

As the poor wretch scrabbled close to me, using his front paws like hands to clutch Forbisher, I could not help but cower.

He sniffled. Like Harry, he even cried without making much fuss. "Aggie, don't be mad at me."

Far off, a voice called, "Little boy! Come back, little boy!"

An enormous, trembling gray paw seized my hand.

The voice seemed to be closer. "Little boy! I have something for you!"

Suddenly, both furry arms were around my neck and the damp snout was snuffling on my shoulder.

Though I shuddered, I made myself remember this was Harry. Removing the arms from around my neck, I struggled to my feet. "Let's get out of here before he finds us."

As that hulk straightened, I saw that he was far, far taller than I. He'd become, not only a monster, but a very large monster.

I heard the voice again. "Little boy!"

I grabbed my brother's paw. "Hurry. Once we're in the van, we can lock him out."

We ran together, away from the voice. Then I saw something I recognized. I snatched it off a twig.

"What's that?" he asked.

"A page from *Mary Poppins.*"

He stopped. "*Mary Poppins*? You tore a page out of *Mary Poppins*?"

"I tore the whole book up!" A monster he might be, but he was still as exasperating as the Harry I knew.

"Wow! What will Mama say?"

"Harry, hurry now and worry later," I urged.

I hadn't stopped to think how a monster this size could hurry. He crashed through the woods, hauling me along so fast my feet touched the ground only part of the time.

Finally, through the trees, I glimpsed our van. Only then did it occur to me what it might do to my sisters to see this creature.

"Wait, Harry. Wait! Wait!" I wheezed.

He ran toward the van, dragging me after him.

Summoning all my breath, I called, "Don't panic! It's only—"

"Aggie?" Emmaline opened the door.

Without even screaming, she collapsed.

Shoving my brother aside, I climbed into the van.

Oralee had yet to glimpse the beast. All she was aware of was Emmaline on the floor. "Aggie, we have to get a doctor! We'd better find a nurse!" Then Oralee saw the beast, our brother, in the doorway. Without a sound, she backed up to a bench, then climbed onto it and stood frozen.

"Harry," I said, "get in here and shut the door!"

As he squeezed into the van, I saw he was wearing a surgeon's gown and mask and carrying a cardboard case with LITTLE NURSE KIT printed on it.

"Sponge!" he snapped, kneeling beside Em.

Oralee stood on the bench, speechless.

"Sponge?" I was as stupefied as she looked.

My brother's gaze wavered for a moment. Then he spoke with all the dignity of a polite rich man who's been insulted by a waiter. "I meant for you." Standing, he lifted me into the sink, cracking my head against the van ceiling, and scrubbed my face with a sponge that appeared in his paw. "Look at yourself. All scratched up and grubby." Taking a damp dish towel from a hook he began to dry me.

Still on the floor, Em moaned.

Dropping the dish towel over my head, the creature rushed back to her side.

Emmaline opened her beautiful eyes. Emmaline opened her mouth.

"Wait!" I clambered out of the sink. "It's Harry!"

The beast turned to me. "Aggie, could you stop calling me Harry? It keeps reminding me how I look." And suddenly, he was the simple shaggy monster again, with no gown, no mask, and no nurse kit.

The anguish that spread through me washed over my astonishment and seemed to dissolve my bones. I sat on the floor beside my brother. I almost forgot that he'd banged my head on the ceiling and draped a damp towel over me.

He *knew* he'd become a beast. My poor, innocent little brother was aware of the frightful change that had come over him. He was not only aware of it, he seemed to accept it, as if he had already exhausted all his shock, all his terror.

"What . . . what should we call you?" I whispered.

"Remember how Mama used to . . . Mama used to call me Rosebud. We could call me that, at least for a little while."

I couldn't speak over the swelling in my throat.

"Rosebud," he murmured. As if from nowhere, a small, cream-colored card appeared in his paw.

Thinking it had to be an illusion, I reached out to touch the card. It was real. I took it. I read it.

ROSEBUD

Secret Agent

FBI

Hastily, I dropped it. "Harry, where did you get that calling card?"

"I think I made it up."

"FBI?"

"Fuzzy Beasts, Incorporated."

I began to suspect that the change in my brother was far, far deeper than mere appearance.

Em sat up. She drew a deep breath.

"Believe me," I told her quickly. "It's Harry."

"Hairy? It's furry!" Her voice was high and shaky. "What is it?"

"Our brother. He's been . . . transformed."

"No!" Oralee shrieked. "It's not! Make it go away!"

"Agnes," Em rasped, "it doesn't even think like Harry. *Fuzzy beasts? Incorporated?* When did Harry ever talk like that?"

"It is Harry," I insisted, "and we can't leave him in this shape."

Oralee's sobs filled the van.

"Oralee." Emmaline was sensitive to noise. "Oralee, think of it as a . . . a handsome prince in

54

disguise. Remember the story of the Frog Prince? Agnes, *get rid of it!*"

"Kiss it!" Oralee wailed. "Turn it into a prince!"

The beast's nose twitched. He shambled over to the stove, on which the last of the split pea soup simmered in a pot. "Oh, boy. Soup!" He bent closer to the steaming peas.

He bent too close.

Roaring, he leaped back. With a furious swipe, he knocked the pot off the stove, sending steaming split pea soup sloshing over the floor.

"Change it! Change it!" Oralee screamed.

"Do something!" Em urged me.

"A prince, please!" Oralee begged.

At that moment, trapped in that forest with a yelping beast before me, nothing seemed more fantastic than what had already happened. Magic, enchantment, spell—what other explanation could there be for this howling monster? And anything was worth a try.

"Harry . . ." I slid to his side through a sea of spilled soup.

"Rosebud," he snuffled.

"Rosebud. Remember the story of the Frog Prince. Concentrate on it." I kissed my fingertips and touched his snout.

The beast disappeared. On the spot where he had stood there crouched a small green frog.

"Oh, Harry!" I moaned. "You got it all wrong!"

"Don't lose him!" Snatching a glass off the sink, Em popped it over the frog.

The frog turned blue. It seemed to grow. It leaped upward with such force it knocked the glass over.

"That does it!" The frog glared at Em a second, then leaped out the open door.

"Harry!" I scrambled out of the van.

Em jumped out after me.

"Watch it!" I cried.

We walked around the van, eyes on the ground, calling, "Harry!"

I scanned the woods around us. "There's no way of knowing which direction he went."

Em put her hand on my shoulder. "Mass hysteria."

"What?"

"Mass hysteria. We've been through so much, losing our way, losing Mama and Harry, being stuck in this awful place, that we've all got mass hysteria."

"You saw him! You heard him! So did Oralee!"

"We thought we did. We all had the same hallucination. That's the power of suggestion. It makes more sense than our brother being a talking frog, doesn't it?"

"But . . . Harry's still gone."

56

She nodded. "We'll mop the soup and find something to eat, and then you can go back out to look for him."

I was so shaken, I wanted to believe her.

I sat on the bench, watching Em and Oralee mop. "If it was mass hysteria, who spilled the soup?"

Oralee picked up Forbisher and shook split peas off him.

I felt as if the van were revolving slowly around me, and my voice sounded thin and faraway. "Em, when Harry ran off yesterday morning, he took Forbisher with him."

For a second, Em looked at me as if she didn't understand me. Then she straightened up and braced her hands against the sink. She closed her eyes and leaned against the sink as if the sink were all that held her up.

"Em, we have to find him."

She took a slow, deep breath. "If a hawk or a fox hasn't got him by now."

"We can't leave him out there!"

Em looked worn and shaky. "We'll have to take Oralee." Kneeling, she put her arms around our little sister. "You're going to be very brave, okay?"

"No," Oralee said.

Em and Oralee and I searched the woods around us. Each time we came upon a page from *Mary*

Poppins I scanned it so I'd remember the order and left it to help guide us, and maybe Harry, back to the van.

We didn't call. "If he's still a frog, that might only make him more jumpy," Em pointed out.

We looked for Harry until the twilight of the forest deepened. Then we heard a far-off voice. "Little boy? Little boy, come see what I have!"

For a minute we stood still. Then Em said, "We have to start back anyway, before it's really dark. Besides, Mama must be there by now. And maybe Harry is himself again, and he's found the van, and they're both waiting for us."

"That's what you said yesterday," Oralee reminded her.

Four

Even with the remaining light, it was hard finding our way back. It was hard, and it was scary, and it must have taken an hour to reach the van. When we did, I saw the glow of a lantern shining through the windows.

"Mama!" Racing past my sisters, I yanked open the door and scrambled in.

A large, fuzzy blue frog crouched on the table, its front legs planted on Em's copy of *Frankenstein.*

The frog looked at me warily. "If she's going to put me in a jar, I won't stay. I only came back because it's getting dark."

Once your brother has become a frog, it's not that much more upsetting to hear him talk.

"It's Harry!" I turned to my sisters. "He's here!"

59

"It's *Rosebud*," he said.

Edging behind Em and Oralee, I shut and locked the van door, in case my brother should take a notion to hop off again. "Harry . . . Rosebud . . . how did you change into a frog?"

"I didn't do it on purpose. You were the one who put the idea into my head."

"Can you change back?" I asked carefully.

He paled to a soft lilac shade. "Don't say that word!"

"What word?" I demanded.

"I can't say it," he whispered.

Em spoke with even more care. "Look, since you're going to stay around, why don't you shift into something more . . . human."

"Why?" he asked.

"For one thing," she snapped, "fuzzy lilac frogs make me nauseous."

"I wouldn't worry about it," he said calmly. "If I'm getting fuzzy, I must be changing again."

He was too calm. Even as I watched, the fuzz was becoming longer, the head was developing ears, and he was sprouting fangs. Yet the transformation didn't seem to upset him. It occurred to me suddenly that being a monster was the most interesting thing that had ever happened to my brother.

"Harry." I tried to keep the panic out of my

60

voice. "Harry, don't. Try to resist. Try—try to get back to yourself again. Remember how *nice* you looked as a little boy."

He gazed at me, and he seemed not at all disturbed to be turning into a hairy beast. "You never told me I looked nice."

"Come on, Harry," I pleaded. "Get serious."

Suddenly, he was the shaggy monster I'd first seen in the woods, but dressed in a dignified gray three-piece suit, black oxfords, white shirt, and navy blue tie. Solemnly, he reached for Em's copy of *The Poems of Percy Bysshe Shelley,* which lay beside him. He flipped through it, as my sisters and I stood dazed.

"Poem," he announced. "Serious poem." Gazing at the book, he recited:

"I arise from dreams of thee
In the first sweet sleep of night.
When the winds are breathing low,
And the stars are shining bright . . ."

Em's hand on my arm was all that kept me from slumping to the floor.

"Agnes!" she whispered. *"Harry can't read!"*

With my sisters, I began backing toward the door, reaching behind me for the handle. Before I could touch it, I heard it rattle, and:

"Little boy? Are you in there?"

The beast leaped off the table to cower on the floor. "Count Backwards!" he whispered.

"Little boy?" The door handle moved again.

"He's not here." I knew counting backward was not going to make the man go away. "Our . . . our mother came back with Sheriff . . . Sheriff Marlowe, and they're out looking for him."

"Sheriff Marlowe?" The familiar voice outside the door sounded surprised.

"Oh, yes," I said.

There was a silence, then, "Well. Thank you. Thank you very much."

We waited, straining to hear some sound outside.

At last, Em whispered, "Do you think he's gone?"

I didn't answer. Our brother, a hairy beast in a business suit, cowered in our camper while outside a terrifying man stalked him.

We waited, the monster huddled on the floor cuddling Forbisher, as the dark outside deepened.

Then I heard in the distance, "Little boy? Come out, little boy!"

"Agnes." Em's hand was cold on my arm. "How did Harry learn to read?"

"I didn't know I could," he said, "until . . . until I did."

Emmaline gripped my arm tight. "He's possessed. That's what it is. See? Now his clothes have disappeared again!"

"You mean . . . something has taken over our brother?" I felt as if a tribe of tiny, icy spiders were marching up my spine.

"No, you idiot!" From her voice, it was plain Em was about to crack. "Our brother has taken over some *thing's* body!"

"But Harry can't read . . ."

"Little boy!" came the far-off voice.

". . . which means he's changed in . . . in . . . who knows how many ways?" I was only scaring myself more.

"Don't tell me more than I want to know," Em warned. "We just have to hang on to him until we can get him exorcised."

"Em, if Harry—"

"Rosebud," the creature said firmly.

"If . . . our brother . . . has possessed some poor beast's body, what we've got here is a beast possessed by our brother, right? So if we exorcise it, we'll end up with the beast and no brother!"

Rosebud stroked Forbisher nervously. "I'm not exercising outside while *he's* still anywhere around."

"If we only knew who that man was," Em said.

"Count Backwards." My brother shivered.

63

"Harry, don't be silly," I said.

"He means the man out there is named Count Backwards." Oralee had been edging closer to the beast.

"Wait. Wait," I breathed. "Harry . . . Rosebud . . . all those hours that man wasn't calling you, *you were with him*?"

"He stumbled across me in the forest," Rosebud said, as Oralee stroked his paw. "I didn't mean to trip him. I was just lying down because I was tired. First he was mad, then he seemed glad to see me, and he said he'd take me to you. Then, when the boat turned over—"

"*Boat?*" I repeated.

"Boat." Oralee settled her brother's arm around her shoulder.

"On a big, dirty lake," he went on. "When I got sick to my stomach and leaned over, the boat tipped. That water was cold! Count Backwards dragged me to shore, but he wasn't very nice about it. When I lost my shoe in the swamp—"

"Swamp." Em's voice was toneless.

"Right after the lake. My shoe came untied and pulled off in the mud, and he said I'd just have to leave it. He carried me a long way, to this gate in a high wall. He put me down, and when the gate opened I kind of got my head caught between the bars. Every time something else happened, he got less and less friendly, but all the time he kept saying what a treasure I was, and then he explained how he was going to clone me."

I was shocked. "Stone you?"

"Comb him." Oralee picked a burr out of our brother's matted pelt.

"*Clone* him," Em interrupted. "To clone something, you take one or two cells from it, and then from them develop hundreds of identical copies of the original thing."

"Hundreds of thousands," our brother muttered morosely. "Count Backwards said hundreds of thousands of me would cause enough Kay somebody to bring the world to its knees."

"Chaos!" Em breathed. "*Chaos.* Oh, Aggie, imagine it! Hundreds of thousands of Harrys running loose in the world! Aggie, with a hundred thousand of Harry, any madman could . . ."

"Rule the world!" I rasped.

"He said we'd have to ruin it first," the beast put in.

I looked at my little brother. Despite his appearance, despite his maddening quirks, I felt a surge of pride and tenderness. "So you ran away from him to halt his fiendish plan!"

"I ran away because I was scared. Besides, he didn't like me. Aggie, being one scared me is awful. Being hundreds of thousands of me scared —that's really scary."

"Oh, Aggie." Em's voice trembled. "*I* told Backwards Harry was a beast. *I* said Harry was a monster who could drive the world crazy. *I* told him the most hideous things Harry had ever done."

"And Backwards figured nobody would suspect sweet, innocent little five-year-old boys. He figured to multiply Harry's . . . Rosebud's . . . genius for wrecking anything he's near by hundreds of thousands . . . No. Wait. Wait." I was becoming more and more baffled with every word I spoke. "If nobody would suspect sweet, innocent little boys, why did Backwards change Harry into this?"

"Aggie," Em's voice was bleak. "Imagine Harry's personality in a hundred thousand of *these.*"

It seemed to me that an army of innocent-looking little boys would be far more likely to take the world by surprise than great horrifying beasts. On the other hand, what did I know about ruining the world? "It's as if he fell into the hands of some Dr. Frankenstein—only a hundred thousand times worse! We have to change him back, somehow, and before Mama sees him."

Oralee, who'd never had a dog or a cat or even a goldfish, nestled closer to our brother. "Change him back? Why don't you go stop Dr. Frankenstone first."

"Oralee," I said, "Dr. Frankenstein lived in Transylvania and that book is fiction."

Rosebud eased Forbisher out of Oralee's reach. "Fiction? *Frankenstein*? Fiction?"

"Fiction," Em assured him. "Made up. Not true."

He clicked his fangs nervously. "Did the lady who wrote it ever say it wasn't true?"

"She's been dead over a hundred years," Em pointed out. "Agnes, one minute he's talking like Harry, the next—"

"Did she ever tell anybody it was not true?" he persisted.

"Harry, how would I know?" Em turned to me. "See? The next minute he's talking—"

"So what do you mean going around telling everybody her book is made up?" He was stern. "I have half a mind . . . half a mind . . ."

"That's it!" Em hit her forehead with the heel of her hand. "That has to be it! Either he is very, very influenced by some of the things he sees and hears, or half his mind is Harry's and the rest is . . . something entirely different."

I heard what sounded like a twig snapping outside.

Em reached to turn off the lantern.

"No!" Oralee gasped.

Em turned off the lantern. "So long as it's on, anybody can see in here."

We sat in the dark with the beast, our brother, listening for any sound outside.

Five

I don't know how long we huddled like that.

Finally, in the dark, I heard Em's voice. "It would never take Mama two days and almost two nights to get back from that town. And she'd never leave us this long unless she's lost or . . ."

"No!" I whispered.

"Aggie, we have to face it. If Backwards has her . . ."

"Why would he clone Mama? With a hundred thousand clones of her, he could only save the world."

"If he has her," Em went on, "it would be a way to lure Harry back. We can't stay here in the van to starve, and we can't leave Mama lost out there or a prisoner of Backwards'. Somebody has to go for help. And somebody has to stay here. If Mama's lost, or hurt, and she finds her way back and we're all gone . . ."

"So. Out there, Backwards is lurking. In here, we're rats in a trap if he breaks in." I heard Rosebud's and Oralee's slow, even breathing, my brother snoring softly. "You can't get far with those blisters," I told Em, "and Oralee can't get far at all. With Harry looking the way he does, only Backwards would dare come near him. I'll have to go with Rosebud while you stay here with Oralee."

It sounded noble, Rosebud and I drawing Backwards away from the van. But I couldn't help thinking that the chances of eluding the man might be better out in the open. Then it occurred to me that we'd walked all over Rosebud's pawprints, and his frog prints, searching for him. In the daylight, anybody could see that the fresh beast prints led away from the van. So we would be doing a noble thing, after all.

Em and I talked it over. We talked the rest of the night, while Rosebud and Oralee slept, without coming up with a better idea.

At first light, I groped for my glasses. "Come on, Rosebud." I shook his hairy shoulder gently. "You want to wash up?"

At least he didn't fall into the toilet this morning.

Emmaline crawled out of bed while I was tying

69

my shoes. "You can't go out there on an empty stomach."

I tied a few slices of bread and an apple in a dry dish towel.

Em looked worried. "What if Backwards is out there?"

"If he's been out all night, he's stiff and cold, so this may be the best time to get away."

Still, it took all my nerve to step outside. I walked around the van, fighting the impulse to dash back inside it. I knocked on the door. "All clear."

Holding Forbisher by a paw, Rosebud stepped out of the van, poking his toe out first, hesitantly, like somebody testing an icy lake. I reached up and took his paw. "It's going to be okay."

We walked back along the road the way Mama had gone. I was terrified that Count Backwards would find us. But I was even more frightened by the idea of coming upon him in the woods. My thoughts were interrupted by a low growling from Rosebud. "Stop that!" I warned.

"It's my stomach, Aggie. I didn't get any breakfast."

I handed him the apple from the towel.

As we walked along the road I heard, faintly, the first normal forest sound, the sound of running water.

Rosebud heard it too. He stopped, sniffing the air. "Aggie, I'm thirsty."

I dreaded leaving the trail for the woods again. "You can wait."

Then, glancing at my brother, I thought how pitiable it was that this great hulking beast, carrying his decrepit teddy bear, had to ask me for a drink.

I led him off the road. As soon as he saw the stream, he let go of my hand. He ran to the water's edge like a charging bear, then flopped on his belly to lap the water. The sight was so startling that it took me a minute to think of germs and water pollution. "Harry—Rosebud—that's enough. Come on, Rosebud. Remember we've got to rescue Mama."

"Rescue?" He stood, dressed in full armor, with a silver helmet over his head. The armor, with his own weight, was more than he could control. He toppled, clanking, into the stream.

"Rosebud!"

Gasping, choking, armor gone, he scrambled out of the creek, clutching the soggy teddy bear, and shook himself like a dog, showering me with cold water. Now that he was safe, I was furious. "Are you out of your mind?" And suddenly I began to understand . . . the nurse kit, the calling card, the frog, the business suit, now the armor . . .

"Aggie, where did that tin suit come from?" He was as astonished as I.

"Out of your mind, I suspect. You know the way ideas just pop into your head sometimes?"

He nodded, sprinkling more water around before I could dodge.

"I think they're popping *out* of your head, Rosebud. We're going to be very, very careful about putting ideas in your head."

He plodded back to the road, clutching my hand and squishing like a giant sponge. His squishing and the dripping from him and the bear were the only sounds in that forest, now.

"At least Count Backwards isn't yelling for me anymore," he said.

My stomach seemed to twist and shrivel. "You're right. We haven't heard from him since last night."

"Good."

"No. He wouldn't just give up. It may mean he has Mama. It may mean he's baiting the trap for you. Think. If he has her, where would they be?"

"Ill Manor, maybe."

"What?"

"Ill Manor. Where he lives. But I wouldn't go near there again for anything."

"It's a lot to expect of me, to save Mama and you without any help at all." I glanced up at him. "You know, you could be a terrifying monster, if you'd just put your mind to it."

He cuddled Forbisher closer. "I don't want to be terrifying. I'm just getting used to how I am now."

There was no use hoping he might stand up to Count Backwards. Hideous as he was, for all his bizarre transformations, his reading poetry, this was still my little brother, who saved leaves and lived to hear the next chapter of *Mary Poppins*. "All right. We'll have to go to town for help."

"That town with everything closed?"

"It's the nearest place I know."

"I have a bad feeling about it. They didn't like us there."

"Whether they like us or not, they have to help us. A sheriff is obliged to enforce the law. Stop dawdling. At this very minute Mama may be lying unconscious in the woods, hidden under a carpet of leaves."

His brown eyes filled with tears.

There was a swishing, swooping behind us, and something nudged our legs so hard we sat. Looking down, I saw we'd been swept up by a carpet.

As it wafted into the air, I braced my hands on either side of me. "How . . . ?"

"You said it." Rosebud hung on to Forbisher and me.

"*I* said . . ."

"You said 'carpet.'"

"Leaves! Leaves! I said carpet of *leaves.*"

The rug rose higher and then soared with astonishing speed over the trees, out of the forest.

"See? See? The carpet *leaves*!" The excitement in my brother's voice was not entirely terror.

I didn't dare dwell on the dreadful possibility that he was beginning to enjoy being a beast. "It's all right, Rosebud. It might even be good." On foot, we couldn't have reached town in a day.

As we flew away from the forest, I tired to think of a way to use my brother's talent safely. "Rosebud, think. We're going to get help to find Mama and capture Count Backwards. We'll make him change you into yourself again. Keep that in mind —or put it out of your mind. I don't know. Just do whatever will make it happen."

In a little while, I saw the town ahead and below.

"They still won't like us, Aggie."

"It doesn't matter. The sheriff will help us find Mama and foil Backwards. You'll be a hero."

Even as I said it, I was beginning to realize the problems we faced. Arriving anywhere with this creature, especially stepping off a flying carpet, how would I be able to explain myself before everybody panicked? How would I be able to explain the beast, ever? I couldn't explain him to myself. How could I hope to convince anyone that inside this ghastly looking brute was a five-year-old boy, my little brother, and, in his heart at least, harmless?

"On the other hand, it might be a good idea to

keep you out of sight until . . ." But I had no good ideas. I could hardly put my little brother off the carpet to wander in this forsaken country. I could never sail into town with him. As it was, I might cause considerable alarm sailing into town by myself.

"Rosebud, wait." Already, we were speeding over the gas station and the town square toward City Hall.

"Wait! Slow down! Stop!" I cried.

The carpet stopped so suddenly Rosebud, Forbisher, and I were catapulted off it.

We landed sprawling on a flat gravel roof. Scraped and sore, I crawled to the edge and peered over.

There was no indication that we'd been noticed. Most people don't go around scanning the sky for flying carpets. In this town, people didn't go around at all. The streets, the square, the air, were soundless and deserted, except for two men who stood on the front steps below, talking.

Rosebud sat up.

"It looks as if we're on the roof of City Hall," I told him. "I have to get downstairs, somehow, without attracting attention. We've got to think of a plan."

"Right!" Plopping on his belly, he pointed over the edge of the roof to the town square.

75

Near the base of the square's statue, poking up through the grass, came an enormous leaf followed by a thick stem.

"Rosebud, I said *plan*!"

The vine snaked rapidly across the street to the front of City Hall, blossoming out with a dozen large, peculiar flowers, then twined up the building's pillars with amazing speed as I stared down. The men on the front steps watched it, like me, transfixed.

As I looked around for the carpet, the vine swept over the roof edge and seized my brother and Forbisher and me in tendrils like steel. Wrapping its leaves around us, it wound its way back down a pillar.

"Look out! Look out!" In a panic, Sheriff Marlowe flailed at the vine.

A tendril whipped around his ankle.

"Here! Stop that! Crazy fool weed!" Raymond Leech struck the vine savagely.

The plant shuddered. Drooping, it let go of Marlowe and seemed to go dormant. The leaf around me was so tight I couldn't move. I could breathe easily, and I realized I should say something to explain my brother, and my predicament. "Help!" I knew, was not the way to calm these edgy men.

Leech peered at the vine. "Dead?"

"I wouldn't trust it." Marlowe rubbed his ankle.

76

Then he bent over Rosebud, Forbisher, and me, lying wrapped like so many cigars in the leaves. "Look at these."

Raymond Leech squinted at us. "This one looks like one of those kids from the hippie van. And that . . . eeyech!"

Shaw came hurrying out of City Hall. "Don't get too close," Leech advised. "They look like pods to me."

"Pods?" Shaw squatted near me. He seemed torn between squeamishness, fear, and fascination.

"There were a couple of movies about pods," Leech told him. "*Invasion of the Body Snatchers.*"

With the toe of his boot, Marlowe nudged Rosebud.

"If anybody around a pod fell asleep," Leech recalled, "pod'd take over his body."

Opening his eyes wide, Marlowe stood quickly. "Better make sure the mother plant doesn't sprout more of 'em."

I felt the vine quiver. As Leech, Shaw, and Marlowe leaped back, it crawled down the steps, then, unfurling its leaves, it dropped Rosebud and Forbisher and me on the sidewalk.

The plant crept across the street, wound around the base of the town square statue, and lay still, its flowers humming softly.

"Kill it!" Leech told Marlowe.

77

"It's pretty fast with those tendrils." Marlowe sounded dubious. "Stalk could whip you around pretty bad."

While I lay half dazed, trying to think of a safe way to break into this conversation, Leech urged, "Shoot it, Shaw."

Shaw took off his mirrored sunglasses. "Where?"

"I'd go for the roots," Marlowe advised.

"Better get rid of the pods first." Shaw nodded toward my brother.

Marlowe gazed at Rosebud. "I don't know. If it's a pod, how would you do away with it so the seeds don't scatter?"

I decided I'd better speak up, then worry about just what to say.

"Excuse me . . ." I croaked.

It's not often a twelve-year-old girl can make grown men recoil in horror.

"They're ready to take over!" Leech cried. "In the movie, they didn't start talking until they were in control!" Drawing Shaw and Marlowe aside, he whispered to them urgently.

Then Shaw and Marlowe sidled into City Hall.

"Don't try anything," Leech warned me. "We've got weed killers that'll put you away in a flash."

"Please." I tried to sound as human as possible. "We're people." I glanced at my brother. "Really. Trust me."

78

"Now!" Leech shouted. "Now!"

Brandishing a spray can, Shaw burst out the door, followed by Marlowe with a rifle.

As Marlowe leveled the gun at my brother, I yelled, "Rosebud, duck!"

Where Rosebud had crouched, there was only a small duck.

"Fly, Rosebud!" I urged.

Fragile, iridescent wings vibrating, a fly skimmed over my head toward the sun.

"Shoot it!" Leech screamed. "Shoot it!"

Marlowe squinted into the sun, but the fly was lost in that glare. Whirling, the man trained the rifle on me.

"I came for help!" I couldn't let go of the hope I could reason with them.

"Put her in with the woman and Chives," Leech snapped.

"Chives?" The only thing I'd ever heard of that was put in with chives was cottage cheese or sour cream dip. I had a mad vision of being crammed into the dairy section of the town's market. "Listen. Let me tell you what happened."

"Up the stairs." Marlowe gestured with the rifle.

With Leech and Shaw leading the way, he herded me into City Hall, then down a flight of stairs.

Leech opened a door with STORAGE stenciled

79

on it, and Marlowe shoved me into a cluttered room. In it was a jumble of mops and brooms and, his wrists tied behind him, a thin, haggard, middle-aged man in a rumpled brown suit sitting on an overturned pail. Beside him, her wrists bound to the back of the chair she sat on was . . .

"*Mama!*" I cried.

"Sit," Leech told me.

"Mama . . ."

"Don't say anything," she warned. "This is a very paranoid group!"

"*Sit!*" Leech commanded.

I sat on the floor beside my mother's chair, facing the only window, a small, barred rectangle high in the wall.

"Put some barricades across the road before any more visitors take a notion to drop in," Leech told Shaw. "I'll radio Beckwids."

Shaw still seemed dazed. "It changed into a duck." He spoke slowly, as if he were trying to convince himself. "I saw it. Did you see it?"

"Just keep your nerve." Leech's voice was steady. "Anything that changes from a pod to a duck is likely to be one of Beckwids' concoctions. Meanwhile, I'd better boil water, plenty of water."

"Water?" Marlowe sounded as confused as Shaw.

"For coffee," Leech said. "You don't dare doze off for a second with a pod around."

"It turned into a duck. Didn't you see it?" Shaw repeated.

"Beckwids," Leech said grimly, "is a pretty odd duck himself. But we're stuck with him."

Six

Sitting beside my mother, I felt hopeless and ashamed, somehow. I'd come here for help in saving my family, only to be taken prisoner.

Marlowe stood cradling the rifle, his back to the window.

"Where are your sisters and Harry?" my mother whispered.

"What happened, Mama, was Count Backwards found him."

"You mean Beckwids?" the man on the pail murmured.

"Beckwids? Who is Beckwids?" I asked.

"Count Beckwids, the master criminal of this loathsome group," the man said.

"I think Backwards must be Beckwids, then," I decided.

"That's enough," Marlowe snapped.

A few minutes later, the door opened and Raymond Leech entered.

Marlowe glanced at him. "No coffee?"

"The kid's not a pod. The . . . uh . . . thing with her was the little boy who came through here in their van."

Mama drew her breath in sharply.

"Come *on,*" Marlowe scoffed.

"I talked to Beckwids on the radio."

"Beckwids did that to a little boy?" Marlowe seemed genuinely shocked.

"Harry got lost in the forest, Mama," I told her, "and Backwards . . . Beckwids . . . found him and took him to his house."

Leech ignored me. "Apparently the boy has a phenomenal talent for creating havoc. I mean, like nothing you ever saw. Right away, Beckwids got the idea of cloning him."

"What would he do with hundreds of thousands of accident-prone little boys running around Eel Manor?"

"That's the genius part." Leech kicked over a bucket and sat down. "Here Beckwids has been fooling around all these years with gene splicing, DNA research, looking to create a life form so horrible we could blackmail the world with it, and then he stumbles across this little boy. Right away, he's cut through decades of research. See, he clones a few of the boy, and we transform some of the empty buildings here into guest houses."

"Guest houses? We bought this town because we needed to be isolated."

"I know. I know."

"You want to turn this place into a nursery school?"

"No, no. Beckwids would keep the little boys at Eel Manor. We'll invite a few travel agents *here* for a free vacation. Treat them like royalty. They'll go home to tell their clients about this undiscovered paradise. People with money love to discover things ahead of everybody else."

I couldn't understand what this had to do with Harry.

Neither did Marlow. "I don't see—"

"It's brilliant. We'll need just a few influential people—university presidents, corporation heads, people with contacts. They'll go back to tell their friends about this marvelous vacation spot. Before long, even more important people will be begging for reservations."

"Diabolical," muttered the captive on the pail next to me.

"Soon," Leech went on, "we'll have generals, ambassadors, senators, bankers. Now, we make one clone of each of *them,* and send each clone home with a clone of the little boy, which they'll pass off as a nephew, or an exchange visitor."

"You're monsters!" Mama exploded. "Monsters!"

Leech was unmoved. "The ambassador clones will bring the little boys to visit their embassies. Military clones will bring them to observe the launchings of space shuttles. Cabinet clones will bring them to the White House. Imagine hundreds of the same incredibly destructive little boy loose in the stock exchange, the United Nations, television stations, and the Kremlin *all at once.* Count Beckwids will be in control of the mayhem. And that is only the beginning!"

I could see it. Hundreds of thousands of Harrys —my forehead felt clammy and my throat felt hot as I pictured them in all those places at once.

Marlowe looked bewildered. "But why did he turn the little boy into that . . . that thing? You couldn't even smuggle that monster into a dog show."

"He didn't mean to. Something went wrong."

"*What?*" Mother and Marlowe demanded at once.

"He's not quite sure. When he was setting up for the cloning, the child bumped into a laboratory cabinet. Phials and specimens, stuff from generations of experiments, smashed all over. Beckwids didn't dare wade into the mess to haul him out. The boy must have figured he was in real trouble, because he bolted before Beckwids could slip on rubber gloves and grab him. Even chasing him across the grounds, Beckwids saw him changing into . . . into a thing that scared the gate into opening."

"Scared . . . the gate?" Marlowe's voice was hushed.

"You know all the work Beckwids has done with robots and artificial intelligence."

"But that thing you say was a little boy—it changes form!" Marlowe reminded Leech.

"Well, you've got all those genes and extracts from tar pits and glaciers and mummies' tombs, along with bacteria and molds and silicon chips. I would say you would definitely call whatever happened a freak accident. Might happen once in a million aeons. It's not necessarily bad, though. Even if Beckwids can't change it back, even if he clones it as it is, we've got hundreds of thousands of a monster that can change into a *fly*. A fly can get in almost anywhere."

Marlowe glanced nervously around the room.

"Anyway, we've got the thing's mother," Leech told him. "Once it gets word that she'll be destroyed in twenty-four hours unless it goes back to Beckwids, it's going to return to Eel Manor. Remember, this is basically a five-year-old kid."

Marlowe wiped his upper lip with his free hand. "What if it comes looking for its sister first?"

"That's why we're taking them all to Eel Manor." Leech stood. "I'll bring a car around front and honk. When you hear the horn, bring them out and right into the car. I'll stay in town in case it does come back."

As Leech went to the door, Marlowe said, "Keep the car windows up. And . . . be sure to shut this door behind you."

I sat, waiting for the sound of the horn. Strangely, it wasn't the thought of my brother as a fly, or cloned as a monster, or even the thought of Mama and me being prisoners, that was most wrenching. It was the idea of my sisters waiting in that van, waiting and waiting.

There was a low howling outside, like the sound-track at the beginning of a vampire movie.

"A sudden strong wind seems to be howling outside," the captive on the pail observed.

Marlowe glanced around the room uneasily. "We don't get winds this time of year."

Through the dirty barred window behind him, I saw a whirl of dust and leaves pinwheel across the square. And sailing past the statue on the gale came a figure . . . such a figure. In one gloved paw it clutched an umbrella. With the other, it steadied a wide, flat straw hat on its head.

As I watched, a shrieking gust sent the creature cartwheeling across the street toward us.

Moments later, I heard the sound of heavy feet in the corridor.

"Leech?" Marlowe glanced toward the door.

"It's the new nanny," came a high, wavering voice from the hall.

"New *what*?" Marlowe seemed close to panic.

"New governess? New housekeeper?" The door was pushed open.

In the doorway stood an enormous hulk wearing high-button shoes, long blue skirt, dark blue coat, and white ruffled apron. The hat perched on its head wobbled with every twitch of the shaggy, gray-blue ears.

Keeping the rifle aimed at us, Marlowe glanced from the corner of his eye at the doorway. With a whimper, he turned the gun muzzle toward the creature, then back toward us, then toward the doorway. I lunged. At the same moment, my mother threw herself forward, chair and all, and Rosebud pounced. As we all collided with Marlowe, the rifle skidded across the floor, and the man in brown planted his foot on the barrel of it.

With Mama's knees on his stomach, my elbow across his neck, and the beast towering over him, Marlowe lay quite still. "All right. All right."

Quickly, I freed Mama from the chair.

"Untie Sir Basil," she told me. "And you, Mr. Marlowe, roll over and put your arms behind you."

Since only the man in brown was still bound, I figured he had to be Sir Basil. I loosed the ropes from his wrists.

Outside, a car's horn sounded.

"You so much as whimper," my mother warned Marlowe, "and we'll send this . . . this *nanny* back to deal with you."

We ran from City Hall, my brother slowing to snatch up Forbisher, who lay sprawled on the sidewalk.

A black sedan was parked at the curb, engine running. Leech was nowhere to be seen. The man in brown slid behind the steering wheel, I got in beside him, and Mama and Rosebud climbed in the back.

We sped across the town square and around the sawhorses that had been placed across the street. Mama touched my brother's snout. "Harry?"

"He wants us to call him Rosebud," I said.

"Oh, he is. He's my baby, my angel." And she cradled that great beast in her arms.

As we roared out of town, Mama asked, "Aggie, where are your sisters?"

"Waiting in the van."

"I hope you told them to wait, no matter what.

I wouldn't want them to head for that town and meet those dreadful characters."

"EVIL." The man behind the wheel drove with a cool but deadly concentration.

"Indeed," Mama agreed. "Hostile, and violent..."

"EVIL," he repeated. "EVIL stands for Eliminate Valid International Laws, or Every Vice Is Legitimate, depending on which of our informants we believe."

"We?" I asked.

"Scotland Yard. Unfortunately, EVIL's suspicions were at a peak when your mother arrived, since they'd captured me only hours earlier."

"It's not your fault," Mama reassured him. "Sir Basil, this is my daughter Agnes, and this is"—her voice trembled—"this is my little boy . . ."

"Rosebud," the beast murmured, cuddling closer to her.

The man nodded, as if he were frequently introduced to hairy monsters. "Chives."

I leaned forward. "Sir?"

"That's correct. Sir Basil Chives of Worcestershire. As in the sauce. I have been tracking EVIL for most of my years with Scotland Yard. EVIL, and Beckwids. His ancestors, as far back as we can trace them, have always meddled in the forbidden, but this present count wasn't content with dark and sinister puttering. No, he allied himself with EVIL early on. But enough of them. Tell me, Rosebud, how did you accomplish that flying feat?"

I glanced uneasily at my brother's back paws, half-expecting to see them sprout wings. But the thought didn't enter his head.

"I don't know," he confessed. "One minute I was a fly, with no mother and no sister and nobody to help us, and I was thinking that Mary Poppins would know what to do."

"What *we* have to do," Mama said, "is save Oralee and Em and warn the people in that town back there."

"There are no other people in that town." Sir Basil's voice was flat.

She was shocked. "You mean they're all . . ."

"No, no. It was practically a ghost town, most of the buildings abandoned. EVIL bought the remaining property, bit by bit, and the few people left there were undoubtedly delighted to sell and move out. Then EVIL spent a fortune restoring the town. We traced a torrent of materials here until a few months ago. That's how I located them, only to be taken prisoner."

"You mean that the whole town . . ." I said.

"Is EVIL's, and no more real than your own Disneyland."

"And I went there for help." Mama leaned forward to stroke my hair. "Oh, baby. If only I hadn't left our van."

Huddled against her, Rosebud told her about Beckwids finding him in the forest, Beckwids' plan to create a hundred thousand Harrys, his escape from the count, and how ideas popped out of his head.

Chives shook his head. "A deadly combination of chance and Beckwids' criminal ingenuity. He's not done yet, you know. The wind may have created some diversion, but EVIL will be pursuing us by now. Our whole escape was part of the trap."

"Trap?" Rosebud's ears twitched.

"Of course. Even Marlowe must have understood that. They would *have* to let Agnes and me escape so we would lead them to you. Even if they lost us, they thought we'd tell you they had your mother at Eel Manor."

Rosebud sat straighter. "My *mother*?"

"What they *didn't* count on," Chives continued, "was your returning to City Hall and rescuing us all." He glanced in the rearview mirror. "But they've recovered from that surprise."

I turned. A black sedan was far behind us, but gaining fast.

"We can drive to the next town and get help," Mama said.

"Unfortunately, they didn't give us enough fuel to get that far." Chives tapped the gas gauge.

"Rosebud," I asked, "could you *imagine* the tank filled with gasoline?"

He tried. He closed his eyes. He clenched his jaw so hard his bottom fangs scraped his snout. Then he asked, "What does gasoline look like?"

"Not much," I confessed.

"Sir Basil!" Mama leaned forward. "There's gas in our van! Keep going down this road."

"Will you know the place where we turned off?" I asked her.

She put a hand on my shoulder. "Honey, I will never forget it." A few minutes later, she said, "I think . . . yes. There, ahead. Turn in that way."

Sir Basil glanced in the rearview mirror. "And none too soon." Tires screaming, he turned onto the forest road. We'd gone little more than a mile when the sedan coasted to a stop. "Empty."

As we leaped out, I said, "The car behind us turned in, too."

"But," Sir Basil said, seizing my hand, "they can't drive around a stalled vehicle."

"Mama," I panted as we ran, "we're leading them right to Em and Oralee. And Beckwids knows where our van is too."

From somewhere above and to the right came the *thwackety-thwackety-thwackety* of helicopter blades. "And," Chives said, "they are not relying on ground pursuit."

Mama drew us off the road. "I've got to try to

get to Em and Oralee before any of those men do," she told Chives. "If I can hide my girls, I'll try to lead at least part of EVIL farther into the woods, and hope you can find help. You all go along, now."

"Mama!" My brother reached for her.

"Honey, you go with your sister. We have no chance at all if we don't split up. Aggie, if . . . if your brother stays the way he is, you do what you can to look after him, hear?"

As she turned away, Sir Basil took my brother's shaggy paw. "Hurry. Our only hope is to melt into the woods."

"Melt . . ." Rosebud looked at him in bewilderment.

"No, Rosebud! No!" I gasped. "Forget you heard that!"

Sir Basil led us deeper into the forest.

When we stopped, finally, I sat with my forehead on my knees trying not to think of my mother and my sisters.

"Can you go on?" Sir Basil asked.

"Where can we go?"

"The last place they'd look for us," he said quietly.

I looked up. "Eel Manor? You think there's a chance we could take Count Beckwids by surprise?"

94

"Not much. But it's the only chance there is."

I got to my feet. "And the only hope of Rosebud ever being a little boy again is to force Beckwids to change him back."

"The only hope," Chives said softly, "is that Beckwids can."

Seven

"How do we get to Eel Manor?" I asked Sir Basil.

"I have no idea. Rosebud, you've been there and come back. If we could find the part of the forest where Beckwids first came upon you, you might be able to reconstruct your route."

My brother scratched his ears. He gnawed his paw claws. He cocked his head to one side, then the other. I noticed that his nanny costume had disappeared.

"*Mary Poppins!*" I breathed. "I left pages from the book stuck all over. If we can find them, we may be able to locate the place where I found Rosebud and work from there."

We searched. I tried not to think about never seeing my mother or my sisters again, or about Harry being a beast the rest of his life. I tried to concentrate every bit of my mind on *looking*.

It took a long time, but it worked. None of us had spoken for what seemed like miles, when I saw a page stuck on a branch. I took it off, and looked at it, and neither my brother nor Chives made a sound.

"Page forty-eight. That means we're getting close to the page where I glimpsed Forbisher."

We came across another page, and another, and at last I said, "This one. I'd just found this one on this twig when I saw Forbisher over there, and then Rosebud came running toward me."

"Can you remember how you got *here*?" Sir Basil asked my brother.

"How I got here . . . How I got here . . ." Holding Forbisher close, Rosebud shut his eyes, concentrating so hard his hair stood out like a porcupine's. "When I bumped into a cabinet at Count Backwards' he got so mad I grabbed Forbisher and ran up a lot of stairs and through the house." He was silent for a minute.

"Then what?" Sir Basil asked.

Rosebud cuddled Forbisher closer and rocked back and forth. "While I was trying to get out of the yard, I felt fur sprouting all over me, and I felt my teeth and my toenails growing. I saw a wall, and the gate opened, and I ran through. I waded across this real gucky . . . you know . . ."

"Bog?" Sir Basil suggested.

"Swamp?" I prompted.

97

My brother nodded. "Yeah. Then I swam the lake."

"You can't swim," I reminded him.

"Now I can."

"There's only one lake in this area," Chives said very quietly. "It's large, dangerously deep, little known, and exceedingly foul. Your early pioneers camped by its shores on their way West, but it was so unwholesome and the land so forbidding, they moved on without even encountering . . ." His voice trailed off.

"Encountering what?" I looked around me.

"There have been Indian tales, legends about a creature in the lake, going back hundreds of years, but no verified sightings. The general eeriness of this place has kept visitors away for centuries, but when you pursue a group as vile as EVIL, you accumulate an astonishing store of unpleasant facts. Go on, Rosebud."

"Once I crossed the lake, I ran into the woods and kept going until I found Agnes." His snout twitched. "I can smell the water from here."

Chives was not cheered. "And you could swim it, and slog through the swamp, because you are seven feet tall, and undoubtedly have the strength of ten men. Agnes and I could not begin to keep up. What you must do is think of some way to get us there with you."

Rosebud tried. He tried so hard tears rolled down his snout.

"I don't think it works when he tries," I said. "Ideas just have to pop out of his head."

"If we can't reach Eel Manor, there's no hope," Chives warned. "If we simply stay here, we'll starve or be captured. If we leave here, we risk being spotted by EVIL. What we have is a vicious cycle."

Hearing a low whine behind me, I turned.

It seemed to materialize slowly, a wavering, insubstantial form at first, then becoming a black, gleaming, utterly sinister-looking motorcycle, with a sidecar attached.

The motor snarled like some stalking panther.

"Splendid." Sir Basil helped Rosebud into the sidecar. "Come, Agnes."

I hesitated. The machine vibrated sullenly, as if it would run me down at the first opportunity.

"Agnes," Sir Basil urged, "we must take advantage of anything your brother can think of. This will at least get around the lake." As I climbed on behind him, he asked, "Which way, Rosebud?"

We hurtled through the forest, dodging rocks and trees, at a speed that would have been thrilling if I hadn't been so terrified. The woods grew deeper, darker, then danker, and the trees began to thin out, until the growth was sparse and scraggly. Finally, through a low fog, I glimpsed the shores of a lake. The grubby sand was littered with bloated toadstools, withered weeds, rotted logs, and skeletons that reminded me of no animal I'd ever seen.

The mists muffled every sound. I could hear, faintly, a helicopter, but there was no way to tell how far away it was, or even from which direction it was coming. Still, the damp clouds around us would hide us from anyone above, and our cycle's low snarling would carry no distance in the fog.

I seemed to hear a great splashing, as if some enormous creature had risen from the water, disturbed by the sound of our passing.

At the far end of the lake, a swamp stretched before us. As we sped along the edge of it, shreds and shrouds of moss, dripping from the branches of dead trees, strayed over my face like ghoulish fingers. In the reeking, vile, bile-green swamp slime I glimpsed what looked like enormous eels, while around them pale swamp snakes swam in slow spirals, threadlike tongues flickering.

The swamp ended. The mist thinned. Ahead of us, a narrow path cut between jumbles of jagged rock. Though the helicopter sounded closer, I didn't dare look up.

There was no way to turn back. The rocks ahead

might shield us. Nobody, I reminded myself, would expect us to head for Eel Manor.

Suddenly, there loomed before us a gray wall of moss-covered stone. Set in the wall was a black iron gate, taller than three of me. As we came closer, I saw on the gate a heavy wooden sign, and on the sign letters of wet, dripping red, which read:

EEL MANOR

Private Property

Beware the Bog

Keep out!

This Means You!

No peddlers or agents

No visitors

By order of

COUNT BECKWIDS

101

Even as I was reading, more letters appeared in streaming scarlet on the sign:

P.S.: Trespassers will be persecuted.

"That should be *prosecuted*," Chives observed. The sign went blank. Every word disappeared. Almost at once a new message painted itself in even wetter, redder letters:

Persecuted.

Persecuted, tortured, tormented,

and otherwise made to feel miserable.

"That's the most unpleasant sign I've ever read." Under his breath, Chives told me, "Keep it occupied. I'll try to find another way in while its attention is focused on you."

UNWELCOME

the sign wrote,

NO SMOKING

Chives edged away to my right, keeping close to the wall.

Though I was not comfortable conversing with a sign, I asked, "Who's smoking?"

Then I noticed that our motorcycle was, indeed, smoking.

CURB YOUR DOG

the sign ordered.

"He's not a dog," I objected.

NO PETS ALLOWED

appeared on the sign.

"He's not a pet," I said. "He is my brother, and he speaks English . . . and he's over seven feet."

The sign went blank. Its wood bleached to white. In large, uneven letters hastily appeared

"That's right," I said.
Immediately came a wild scrawl:

NO CENTIPEDES!

"Seven feet is his height," I explained. Without Chives, I realized how alone my brother and I were, and how reckless we were to have come to this dreadful place.
Shaking, barely legible letters quivered across the wood now:

ON VACATION

OUT TO LUNCH

LOST OUR LEASH

CLOSED FOR REMODELING

SEVEN FEET?

104

Letters came in a frantic rush:

We refuse the right to reserve nervous

In emergency break grass

Keep off the glass

DO NOT CROSS GO

Do not grow cross

NO GO

no no no no

and, finally, in tiny, pale, exhausted scratches:

. . . help . . .

There was a screech of metal scraping stone, and
the great gate began slowly to open.

I heard a helicopter behind us, closing low and
fast.

Our cycle shot through the gate and demateria lized, leaving me sitting first on nothing, then on the ground.

"Agnes." Rosebud was sprawled beside me. "We're in Count Beckwids' yard."

I didn't want to look around too closely. "Front or backyard?"

"Graveyard."

Eight

The helicopter passed over us, then descended somewhere beyond a stand of willows.

My brother began scratching a hole with his front talons. "Hide. Hide. Hi—"

I followed his gaze. Among the tombs and slabs and monuments, Count Beckwids stood, wearing a black tuxedo and cape. As he approached us, he bared those tiny white teeth in a cold smile.

Rosebud scrambled to his feet, brushing dirt from his snout. Then, glancing down at the hole he'd made in the graveyard, he shuffled his feet, trying unobtrusively to sweep the earth back in the cavity. With one paw, he clutched Forbisher. With the other, he squeezed my hand. "Courage," he whispered. "Control yourself. Don't let him see you're afraid. They can scent fear, these savages."

With the paw that held Forbisher, he tried to brush dirt off me. "Children." He smiled feebly at the count. "Wretched little beasts. Still, what would we do without them? Straighten up, Agnes. We must hurry home. Mother will be frantic."

Beckwids surveyed my brother from the tips of the ears that peeked out below a pearl-gray top hat to the front paws clad in gray gloves. "How long have these . . . materializations . . . been happening?" the count asked me.

I couldn't even manage to shrug.

"How long has he been talking that way?" Beckwids asked. When I didn't answer, he reached for my arm. "Speak up!"

"Off . . . off and on," I quavered, "ever since . . . we got him back like this. He's terribly influenced by anything he . . ." Then I realized I wasn't sure whether the way Rosebud had just spoken was affected by memories of *Mary Poppins* or by Beckwids himself.

"Fascinating." The count eyed my brother with interest. "It would seem that whatever happened to you in my laboratory is causing some brain cells to mature more rapidly than others, but in haphazard, unbalanced fashion. You are an incredible monster. I must keep a few of you for study. But we can't let you out anymore. You'd be certain to attract attention prematurely, and perhaps lead it to us. Which you have done." Beckwids gazed at me.

"Which you have done." He tightened his hold on my arm. "But since you're here, we must find some use for you."

His grip unrelenting, he led me through the graveyard, my brother clutching my other hand.

The front garden of Eel Manor was dotted with trees and bushes trimmed into bizarre, unnatural shapes. The grass itself was a dazzling, unwholesome green.

The house was of stone, three stories high, with turrets and towers, and windows that resembled dead, blank eyes. As we approached, the front door groaned open, then slammed shut once we'd stepped inside.

My brother bared his fangs in a tremulous grin. "Lovely visit. So good of you to have us. Pity we can't loiter, but we must run before we're late for tea. Teatime, Agnes. Teatime!"

"We'll have tea downstairs." The count's hand was cold and merciless. He led Rosebud and me to a staircase, down a flight of wide stone stairs, down another flight, and another flight lit by flickering torches set in serpent-shaped sconces attached to the damp walls.

At the bottom of the steps, he led us down a long, cold tunnel. Moss oozed from between the stones of the wall. The tunnel ended abruptly, leaving us facing a steel door.

Beckwids drew a rusty key from his vest pocket

and tried to insert it in the lock of the massive door. The key wouldn't turn. The count muttered in annoyance, felt in an inner pocket of his coat, and found another, smaller key.

My brother cleared his throat. "Agnes and I have decided that whatever we came to discuss with you is not worth the trouble."

"No trouble." Beckwids tried the second key, tossed it over his shoulder, and patted the pockets of his trousers.

"Trouble," Rosebud muttered, glancing wildly around him. "Trouble, trouble, trouble."

"Stop that!" commanded the count.

Cringing, my brother buried his snout in Forbisher's fur. I was too terrified to comfort him.

"Do you know how distracting it is to have a monster muttering at you?" Beckwids demanded. "Do you know how hard it is for me, coming down here day after day for experiments, trying to develop all my plans and plots?" He turned the knob and the door opened. "There now," he growled. "You must have been unlocked all the time." He pulled me through the doorway, with Rosebud clutching my hand.

"You see what I have to contend with?" Beckwids asked me. "Nothing but androids and robots to tend the house and grounds, nothing but this ridiculous muttering beast with which to destroy civilization and rule the world. Unless, of course . . ."

The door clanged shut behind the three of us.

"I don't like that." Rosebud handed Forbisher to me. "I don't like that door clanging shut behind us."

There was no knob, no handle, on our side of the steel door. Rosebud pushed at it with his shoulder. He scratched it with his paw claws. He raked it with his toe talons. He bent his head to the side and bit at it, until I saw nothing of my brother in him, only a monster.

Then he stopped, took Forbisher from me, and turned to Beckwids. "Excuse me. Your door doesn't open."

Beckwids scowled at my brother. "Look at you. Do you know how ridiculous you are, a hideous beast carrying a stuffed toy?"

"This old thing?" But Rosebud held Forbisher closer.

We were in an enormous room. Along two of the steel walls were shelves and cabinets, and on the shelves were jars full of fluids, powders, bits of tissue, things I didn't want to look at for too long. Lining another wall were rows of machines, monitors and computers, and tables with tubes and phials, cruets, and Bunsen burners. All the machines were humming and all the liquids in the tubes were burbling and hissing.

In the center of the room was a long, stainless steel table with straps at both ends. At one side of it was a smaller table with an array of scalpels, scissors, saws, and syringes laid out.

In a far corner, I noticed what looked like the skeleton of a large, unsteady, badly constructed animal.

Beckwids saw me staring at it. "An early effort."

"This looks like a laboratory, or a surgery," I observed uneasily.

The machines hummed and hissed louder and the liquids gurgled like laughing trolls.

"Quiet!" Beckwids snarled.

The humming and hissing and gurgling stopped and the room was silent.

Rosebud took a deep breath. "Uh . . . I just remembered. There's this mad doctor Frank something in some sylvania. I think Agnes and I were supposed to go there."

The count looked almost wistful. "Transylvania. My family home for generations. Wonderful place. Fens and forests, fogs and bogs, crypts and catacombs, mists and moors." Removing his cape, he hung it on a hook, then went to a cupboard.

"So why did you leave?" The only hope, I knew, was to distract the count and hope that Sir Basil had found a way in.

"My father got into a little trouble with the law there." Beckwids filled a syringe from a small bottle.

"For what?" I felt as cold as the walls around us.

Beckwids only smiled. "With my father imprisoned, I took his records, his materials, and moved to the New World."

"You left your father in prison?" I could not hide my astonishment.

"He was eventually released for bad behavior."

"*Bad* behavior?" In spite of myself, I was interested.

"Oh, yes. He was so unpleasant no prison would keep him."

"He's still in Transylvania?" Until that moment it had not occurred to me there might be things more sinister than EVIL or Beckwids lurking about Eel Manor. I moved close to my brother.

"Still." The count placed the syringe on the long steel table. "Of course, he's quite ancient now. He keeps busy making the old reliables—battery-operated toys that drain the batteries in a few hours, electric trains that fall off the track on the curves, leaky Thermos bottles, automobiles that break down after midnight on weekends, computers that—"

"Did . . . did any of the stuff my brother got into come from Transylvania?" In spite of myself, I couldn't help thinking of werewolves and vampires—I couldn't put out of my mind the flash of pure monster in the way my brother had attacked the door.

"From Transylvania?" Beckwids repeated. "Oh, yes. But even I have no idea where some of the substances came from originally. Our family has been experimenting with life forms for centuries. There were bits of failed efforts, chunks of meteors . . . who knows what genes may have been latent in *them*?" He smiled. "What a lovely joke, to imbed material from the most absurd combination of creatures in a meteor and hurl it into another galaxy, knowing it might be found and extracted. But your brother must have been splashed by the contents of hundreds of phials, some my ancestors never even labeled. He may have been infected with rare, even extinct earth species, traces of Bigfoot, Abominable Snowmen. . . ." He gazed at my brother. "All the years I strove to create a living being, I had no luck."

"Why go on trying?" I had to keep talking, keep Beckwids away from the scalpels and my brother, and hope Sir Basil had found his way in.

"Family tradition. And to show up my father. Oh, he had his grandiose plans, but he's an old-fashioned man, really. I doubt if he knows a laser from a quark. And yet, with all my new ideas, new technologies, I'd had only failures when you misplaced your brother practically in my lap. What incredible luck." He rearranged his scalpels and syringes. "In the first hours, he wrenched my knee, capsized my boat, nearly drowned me, and caught his head in my gate. He no sooner stepped into my graveyard than he tumbled into an empty grave."

"Whose?" I whispered.

"One never knows who may drop in," Beckwids murmured, then returned to his narrative. "Entering my house, your brother tripped over the hall runner and smashed a priceless funeral urn. At dinner, he spilled wine on a hundred-year-old tablecloth—"

"You gave my little brother wine?"

"Well, I didn't set out expecting to find a five-year-old catastrophe. My sensors picked up a vehicle entering the forest, and when my robot patrols wouldn't start, I went out to investigate, met you and your sisters, and then him. Just *one* little Harry has shattered my nerves. Imagine hundreds of thousands of him loosed on the world."

"Then you're going to change him back to a little boy." In my relief, I forgot the rest of our problems, for the moment.

"Oh, I hope I can. First I'll clone a few dozen of him as he is. Then, with a good supply of him, I'll try restoring some to the little wretch he was. That way, it will be no great loss if I . . . bungle a few."

They would all be my brother, I realized. Dozens of Rosebuds, maybe a few Harrys, and—whatever the bungled few turned out to be, they, too, would be my brother.

There was a clanging at the steel door. Beckwids pressed a button beside the operating table and the door opened.

"No!" I cried.

Nine

Sir Basil Chives stood disheveled and haggard, his arms gripped by Leech and Marlowe. As they dragged him into the laboratory, a tea cart followed them silently.

"I never would have believed it," Marlowe said. "Eel Manor is the last place I would have expected them to go."

Beckwids smiled thinly. "Which, as I told you, is precisely why they came here. That is why I am a genius, and you're not." As the cart stopped before Beckwids, he lifted the lid of a silver teapot and peered in. "Well, you've let it steep too long again," he accused the cart.

"What are we going to do with Chives and the girl?" Marlowe asked.

"I'll test various combinations of the material the

boy got into on her," the count said. "Since she's related to him they should affect her the same way. If we can reproduce whatever happened to him we can try to reverse it."

Until that moment, it had seemed to me that having my little brother a beast, or cloned, was the most dreadful thing that could happen. But becoming a monster myself was a horror so vast I couldn't imagine it.

"No word from Shaw?" Beckwids asked.

"Not since he went after them by car when they escaped. From the helicopter, we saw him follow them on to the forest road. The mother may have gone back for her other girls, but they'll never get past Shaw," Leech said.

I heard them, but it seemed as if I were somewhere outside of myself, not really connected to this place or these people.

"What about Chives?" Marlowe asked Beckwids again. "You told us to make him talk. Biggest mistake you ever made."

Chives was calm. "I am Sir Basil Chives of Worcestershire—Worcestershire, as in the sauce. I am on special assignment for Scotland Yard, tracking the count and EVIL, which, of course, you may have surmised."

"You see?" Marlowe demanded. "That's what we've had to contend with."

"You're not supposed to tell everything, just like that," Beckwids admonished the detective. "You're supposed to force them to force you to talk."

"But that would be so unpleasant," Chives objected, "and I'd be no good for anything afterward."

What if I turned into a shaggy beast like Rosebud? What if the experiments on me would be so bungled I'd be recycled into one of Beckwids' androids, as useful as the gate or the tea cart?

"You tell us to find out what Chives knows," Marlowe accused Beckwids, "but you don't have to listen to him go on and on."

What if I became something with no memory of my mother, with no memory of *myself*?

"I know you're planning to clone this girl's brother," Sir Basil continued. "I know Leech and Marlowe and Shaw are EVIL, which stands for—"

"We know what it stands for," Leech interrupted irritably.

Rosebud stroked Forbisher anxiously.

"I know you all moved to this remote area, from which you planned to forward your schemes for world domination," Chives went on.

"See? See?" Marlowe was becoming even more upset. "He keeps telling us what he knows, but everything he tells us we already know."

"I might as well clone him, then," Beckwids said. "I can always use the practice."

"Are you crazy?" Marlowe demanded, and then flushed as Leech shook his head warningly. "I mean, think of it—a hundred thousand Chives telling us everything he knows we know."

"No, no," Beckwids said. "I'll make just one clone, to infiltrate Scotland Yard. But first I want a few dozen clones of the beast. I'll keep several of him as he is for study, or maybe for terrorizing a population or two. Then, in case anything goes wrong with the girl, I'll still have plenty of him left."

I edged toward the cabinets, thinking that I might be able to grab a few bottles dangerous enough to hold Beckwids and EVIL at bay.

"No, you don't." Marlowe seized my shoulder from behind.

"Better find Shaw and the rest of her family," Beckwids told Leech. "Come along, Harry."

My brother backed into a corner, clutching Forbisher.

"Come!" the count commanded. "And put down that stupid teddy bear."

Harry slid to the floor, holding Forbisher tighter.

I tried to wrench free, but Marlowe pinned my arms behind me.

"Stand up, beast!" The count's voice was venomous.

My brother only whimpered.

Snatching Forbisher from Rosebud's paws, Beckwids twisted the old bear's neck viciously.

My brother howled.

I've never heard a sound like it. That howl was pure monster, pure beast, a shattering cry of sadness, of desolation, despair, torn from the heart of all the galaxies.

Marlowe recoiled as if he'd been struck. The tea cart shivered. The cups and saucers on it clinked. Even Leech looked shaken.

"Stop that!" Beckwids thrust Forbisher at my brother. "Here. Take it!"

Cuddling the old bear close, Harry stroked its worn fur.

"You must never howl like that again." Beckwids attempted to pour a cup of tea, but his hands trembled so he set down the cup and saucer. "If you should howl like that while I'm cloning you, there's no telling *what* might happen."

My brother sniffled.

Beckwids reached for him. "Get Chives and the girl out of here until I'm ready for her," he told Leech.

Ten

Marlowe and Leech took Chives and me to a small room at the end of a corridor. We were silent, all of us, left solemn and unnerved by my brother's dreadful howl.

Beckwids' tea cart followed us.

Leech took a scone from the platter on the cart. With his pocket knife, he spread marmalade on the scone, then set the scone down without tasting it. He poured a cup of tea and stood looking into the cup.

I wondered if I would ever see my brother again, either as a shaggy beast or as a little boy—and I realized the beast was as much a brother to me as the child.

Marlowe's voice was subdued. "We were supposed to do something." He looked uncertainly at Leech.

"Help Shaw round up the girl's family," Leech told him absently.

"Right. Right. Now?"

"Now. Yes." Leech still held the cup and saucer, making no move to drink, still shaken by that howl.

I knew that if I tried to run, one of them would catch me before Sir Basil could do anything.

"So where's her family?" Marlowe asked.

"I don't know," Leech snapped.

"What if they scattered?"

"Then they have to be collected one by one." Leech put his cup back on the cart.

My brother's howl seemed still to hang in Eel Manor. While it had left Leech drained and preoccupied, it seemed to have made Marlowe so nervous he had to keep moving, talking, acting. Standing over my chair, he glowered down at me. "Where are your sisters? Where did your mother go?"

"He's just a little boy," I said. "How can you do such things to a little boy?"

Chives interrupted. "Did you hear that?"

"I heard her," Marlowe seemed almost ashamed.

"No, *that*!" Sir Basil said.

I heard it then. I heard it and felt it, a *thud-thud* that grew louder and seemed to come closer even as I listened.

Thud-thud-thud. Something that sounded like a monumental pile driver was advancing toward Eel Manor.

123

None of us moved.

As the pounding came closer, the floor beneath us shook.

Beckwids staggered into the room, steadying himself against the walls like a man trying to walk through an earthquake. "I *told* you I must never be upset while I'm working!"

"Where is my brother?" I cried.

The *thud-thud* drowned out my voice. The walls around us groaned. Then the sounds stopped.

Beckwids looked up. "It . . . it was from *outside*! Leech, go see what it is."

"I'm not going up there." Leech gripped the edge of the tea cart, which had moved closer to him.

"I wouldn't go up there," Marlowe agreed.

"*You* go up there," Leech told Beckwids.

Beckwids gazed at him a moment, the doll-blue eyes unblinking, then whispered in a voice so venomous that even Chives flinched, "All right. I'll go up there."

The count strode from the room.

"What do we do now?" Leech's voice broke the hush.

"You were telling me to make the girl talk, but I'd just as soon wait."

I thought of my little brother left alone in that laboratory, or, worse, becoming many shaggy beasts.

There was a crash upstairs, and the room seemed to rock under the impact. As I leaped to my feet, neither Leech nor Marlowe moved to stop me.

"Would you happen to know if this place has a basement exit?" Marlowe asked Chives.

There was another crash, and the sounds of wood splintering and glass breaking, as if a whole wall were disintegrating.

Leech ran from the room, followed by Marlowe.

Quickly, I untied Sir Basil's wrists, then dashed toward the laboratory with Chives at my heels.

Eleven

Beckwids had left the laboratory door open.

My brother lay strapped down on the operating table, a sheet over his great shaggy body. I could not tell whether he was breathing. "Harry . . ." I whispered.

He didn't move.

I ran to the table. Though his eyes were open, he made no sound. But the gaze was the soft, worried gaze of my little brother. Kneeling, I unbuckled the straps. Then—I had to know. "Rosebud, are there any more of you?"

He sat up and threw his arms around my neck, bending my nose.

I seized his arms. "Rosebud, *did he operate*?"

My brother shook his head, knocking my glasses awry. "He'd just picked up a knife when some big

126

loud footsteps outside made me jump, and I kind of bumped his hand so he dropped the knife. Then he got all mad and said he'd have to sterilize everything again, and stomped out."

"Oh, Rosebud." I threw my arms around my little brother. "I love you."

"So can I get out of this dumb white nightgown?"

Chives picked up a scalpel and handed me another. "There's no telling what we may encounter. Rosebud, is there a basement exit?"

"I don't know. I went up a lot of stairs the other time I got out of here." Sliding off the table, my brother picked Forbisher up from the floor.

"We'd better try the way you know," Sir Basil said.

There was a crash from somewhere above. Then the house groaned. At the next crash, the cabinets lining the walls of the laboratory quivered. As their doors swung open, bottles on the shelves toppled and smashed.

The burbling and hissing in the tubes and cruets on the tables stopped for a second, then resumed at a frantic pitch.

I grabbed my brother's paw and, with Sir Basil, we dashed from the room. As we ran, trying to retrace the route we'd been brought to the laboratory, there was an impact above that made the stone walls around us shake. Then, with a long, low roar, they collapsed. Ahead, a slab, loosed from the ceiling, fell in a rain of mortar.

Choking, half blinded by mortar dust, we stumbled past the stone.

Finally, through the swirling gray cloud, I glimpsed a flight of stairs and, beside it, an enormous green pillar. As we reached the steps I paused, fighting for breath. "Looks like . . . some stairway . . . but the one we came down didn't have a pillar. . . ."

Even in that roiling gloom, I could see this was a most peculiar pillar. Green and scaly, it stood on a splayed, three-toed base and extended up through a great, irregular hole in the ceiling.

Coughing, Sir Basil leaned against the pillar, then leaped back. With his mask of dust, his red-veined, staring eyes, he looked like some tribal mask. "It's alive!" he rasped.

My brother's furry ears flattened back against his skull.

The pillar twitched, which, in something that massive was like the shifting of a monument.

"It's a leg!" Chives gasped. "Rosebud, why in heaven's name did you think up *that*?"

"Me?" My brother clutched Forbisher tight. "I could never think of anything like that."

There was a momentary stillness, like the endless instant after a bus collision or an auto wreck, the instant before you hear broken glass hit the pavement.

Chives' whisper was urgent. "Are you sure there's no other way out?"

My brother only clung to his bear.

"And no way back," Chives said.

Rosebud's furry paw tightened on my hand. "Aggie?"

I looked up at his damp black nose and his timid brown eyes.

The corridor behind us was sealed off. The leg twitched again and we were showered with debris from the floor above.

I had my little brother to look after.

"If the staircase goes . . ." Chives muttered.

I nodded. ". . . we'll be buried down here."

"We can only hope, then . . ."

". . . that whatever belongs to that leg stays put. So we'd better hurry." I squeezed my brother's shaggy paw and led him to the foot of the stairs.

As I looked up the steps, gathering my nerve, Sir Basil said, "Go ahead, now."

I turned to him. "But you might not get . . ."

He smiled. "Look at it this way—you'll be the first to meet the owner of that leg."

"Aggie . . ." Rosebud edged even closer to me. "If it's too scary . . ."

"I'll tell you so you can shut your eyes." Just saying it used up a large part of my courage.

I started up the stairs.

I guess, sometimes, in a crisis, your mind just starts working, clear and focused, like a cool, wise friend.

All the way up, flight after flight, my mind was coaching me:

Whatever the creature is, it's too big to manage a sideways kick. Keep moving. If it ever tried to kick sideways, it would topple. IF IT SHOULD TOPPLE . . .

Whatever you do, don't think about the creature toppling. Don't look at the leg. Keep moving. Okay. Only a few more flights. Don't look at the leg! HOW TALL IS THAT LEG? Forget the leg! Just concentrate on climbing.

Okay. Rest a second. Only a couple more flights. Keep climbing. Good.

WHAT A CRASH! How can the house stand up?

Wait. Let the stairs stop shaking.

Now. Don't try to run. Don't stumble. One step —another—almost there—

From somewhere above, I heard Beckwids' voice. "Here! Stop that!" Then he screamed.

I stopped.

Mama said to look after Harry.

"You! Down there!" Beckwids' voice was shrill.

"If you thought this up, little boy, you had better think again!"

I climbed, knowing I would have to face whatever was destroying Eel Manor.

At least, the thing seemed in no hurry to silence the count. As I climbed the last steps, I heard him shriek again, then shout, "You! Stop loitering down there! Come get rid of this loathsome reptile! Ah, there! It's munching my African violets. Filthy brute! Take that! *Help!*"

I reached the foyer of Eel Manor and groped for my brother's paw. The weight of the invader had sent one leg through the floors below it, the body had knocked out several walls, but the thing stood placidly in the wreckage, neck stretched along the front hall, head in the parlor.

Maybe I'd been through so much that I saw things differently. Maybe I'd spent all my fear. Maybe the size of the creature was so overwhelming that terror was too feeble a response to the sight of it.

People who have come close enough to touch a whale in wonder report feeling awed and joyful.

People *expect* a whale to be in the ocean.

A dinosaur does not belong in a manor house, not in this century.

The awe I felt was something no whale watcher

could imagine. There was no joy in it, but neither was there fear.

Maybe because my own brother was a beast, I could sense what kind of a monster this was. For all the havoc this dinosaur had created, I knew, with no idea how I knew, that only its dumb plodding bulk destroyed anything. There was no more menace, no more malice, in that reptile than in a whale. I knew all this though I couldn't see into the parlor to look the beast in the face.

Almost absentmindedly, I moved so Sir Basil and Rosebud could join me. "It won't hurt us," I said. "Not on purpose."

Though we couldn't see Beckwids, we heard his shouts from the parlor.

"Put me down! Down, I say!"

There was a tinkling like a shower of broken light bulbs, then, *"Not up here!"*

With no way to get around that enormous hulk, we could only make our way beside the neck, careful not to brush it as we sidled toward the front door.

As we came abreast of the parlor, I saw that the head was nibbling a potted fern.

Beckwids was perched precariously on a chandelier while Leech and Marlowe crouched in the fireplace. The iron grillwork at the windows swung loose, the panes shattered. In that shambles, the broken glass scattered over the wreckage shone like midnight frost.

Wondering how to get past the creature's head without attracting attention, we hesitated.

"Home! Go home!" Beckwids pitched a few chandelier crystals at the dinosaur.

The behemoth swung its head slowly toward us.

Chives remained calm. "Prehistoric, plainly. Obviously a close relative of the brontosaurus. Contrary to popular belief," he continued, as the great head moved closer to my brother, "the brontosaurus was a peaceable vegetarian. I suspect your howl called it up from the depths, Rosebud."

"From the *deaths*?" Rosebud whispered.

Stricken, Beckwids stared down at my brother. "Rosebud? *Rosebud?* I was going to rule the world with a beast called *Rosebud*?"

Sir Basil patted my brother's shaggy shoulder. "The depths, lad. The deepest waters of the lake. The howl you howled in the count's laboratory was the cry of a primal soul, older than most of us can imagine, from a time before the dawn of speech, or man, or reason. Imagine this saurian, undoubtedly the last of his kind, lurking in dark waters aeon after aeon, alone and forgotten. He hears a cry that stirs ancient memories . . ."

"What you are saying," Beckwids snarled from the chandelier, "is that it takes one to know one."

Chives clambered over the reptile's neck into the parlor. "It is time to take these blighters into custody."

"Yes." My brother nodded. "Yes, it is. What's a blighter?"

"EVIL and the count," Chives said, handcuffing Leech to Marlowe. "Beckwids, drop down here. And I warn you, this prehistoric creature senses his kinship with Rosebud. Should any of you offer the slightest resistance, we will not attempt to restrain the reptile. Peaceable it may be, but it is plainly loyal to its own kind."

Without a word, Beckwids let go of the chandelier and dropped to the floor. Then he stood quietly while Chives bound his arms with drapery tiebacks. "Now," Sir Basil told my brother and me, "we must lure the brontosaurus back to its natural habitat and transport these felons to justice. Rosebud, as soon as I get EVIL and Beckwids out the windows, you and Agnes may come out the front door. I'm sure the reptile will follow."

It did. It followed Rosebud out, plodding right through the front wall of the house.

We had no trouble finding EVIL's helicopter. Stumbling, glancing in terror at the dinosaur, Leech and Marlowe led us through the graveyard to a landing pad.

"Rosebud," Chives said, "you might lend a paw here."

Handing me Forbisher and patting the dinosaur's neck, my brother hastened to help. He climbed into the craft, then hoisted Leech and Marlowe and the count and me in.

As Chives settled himself in the cockpit, I couldn't help asking, "Have you ever flown before?"

"Many years ago. I'm sure the principles haven't changed."

I closed my eyes as he fumbled with the controls.

"What about my dinosaur?" Rosebud sounded worried.

"He'd never fit," Chives said gently.

I heard the *choppity-choppity* of the blades and felt the machine rise. When I looked down, we were passing over the wall that surrounded Eel Manor.

Below, the brontosaurus plodded through it.

By the time we reached the swamp, the reptile was lagging behind us.

"He's not keeping up!" Rosebud warned.

"He'll make his way back to the lake," Sir Basil assured me.

"Rosebud," I said, "he'd never be happy out of his home."

So, after hearing my brother's cry, seeking him

out, and following us, the lake monster was abandoned, and alone again. To take my mind off the dinosaur, I asked Chives, "What about EVIL and the count?"

"They'll be locked up for a long time," he assured me.

"How about if we make them turn Eel Manor into a nursery school?" my brother proposed. "There's a lot of really neat stuff there, especially now that it's wrecked. And they wanted a hundred thousand of just *me.*"

Beckwids' moan ended in something like a sob.

Before long, I saw the forest below us, and then the narrow road and the top of our van. As we hovered over it, my sisters and my mother climbed out, then Shaw, holding a gun.

"Mama!" My brother leaned out of the helicopter so far he dropped Forbisher.

As I grabbed Rosebud, Shaw put up an arm to ward off the plummeting bear. My mother must have thought he was aiming at her son, because she whirled, knocked the gun aside, then struck Shaw a great blow to the side of his head with her fist.

"Ladder . . . ladder . . ." Chives said. "Ah!" He pulled a lever, and a ladder dropped out the helicopter door.

Before the ladder was fully unfolded, Rosebud

was scrambling down it. "Mama!" Even before his foot-paws touched the bottom rung, he let go, landing on Shaw.

"Hurry, Agnes," Chives urged, "while there's anything left of Shaw to rescue!"

Though I was scared and dizzy climbing down that swaying ladder, I called out, "No, Mama! Save him for the law!"

After being struck by a falling teddy bear, attacked by our furious mother, and landed on by a shaggy beast, Shaw couldn't even summon the nerve to climb to safety. We had to wait for Chives to lower a sling.

"If he gives you a minute's trouble, you just send him back here," Mama shouted as the whimpering Shaw was hauled aboard the craft.

It circled once, in farewell, and then flew east.

Twelve

So we found ourselves where we had been days earlier, stranded in the forest. Only now we were out of food and trapped by two cars behind us.

We climbed into the van. Mama hugged and kissed us all again and sat stroking Rosebud's paw while he and I recounted everything that had happened since we left her.

"Mama," I said finally, "people would never believe any of this."

"Not unless they saw Harry," Em observed. "Anybody who saw Harry would believe anything."

I gazed around us. "Anyway, here we are."

"Here we are," Em repeated, "trapped and starving, with night falling."

"It's not even twilight," I told her.

Mama put her hand on my arm. "Let her be, Aggie. She's earned a grumble."

"Mama," Rosebud asked, "isn't there even any soup left?"

She stood. "Come on, sweetie."

We walked back along the road, Mama and I followed by my sister and brother, Oralee holding Rosebud's paw.

"Harry," I heard Em whisper, "I never meant ..."

I turned.

My brother shifted Forbisher higher under his arm and rested a furry paw on Emmaline's shoulder.

I turned away. When somebody like Em tries to apologize, it's not right to intrude.

Shaw had left his car parked behind the black sedan.

"*Gorgeous!*" Em breathed as she climbed in.

"Don't get attached to it," Mama said firmly. "We're only going to take it back where it belongs."

I have never heard an engine that quiet, nor sat on seats so soft.

As we backed out of the forest road, Oralee looked worried. "We're not going to just leave our van?"

"We'll figure a way to get it out of there," Mama promised. "The first thing, though, is to get you all fed."

"The nearest grocery is at EVIL's town," I reminded her. "That's a long drive."

Mama glanced at Rosebud. "Don't even think of any fancy travel notions. Nobody in this family is doing any more flying around with umbrellas and long skirts."

"We have to leave word for Sir Basil so he'll know we drove back to EVIL's town," I said.

On the dirt road we'd just backed out of there appeared in huge fluorescent letters:

WORD

FOR SIR BASIL

WE DROVE BACK TO EVIL'S TOWN.

"I guess, with him reading, I shouldn't be so shocked that he can spell," Em murmured.

I slept for most of the trip. When the car stopped, I opened my eyes, groggy and disoriented.

We were parked on a deserted street, my brother snuggled against me, Forbisher in his arms.

If that town had been eerie in the daytime, it was unearthly at night, like a set from an old "Twilight Zone" segment.

"It just doesn't seem right," Mama said.

"It doesn't even seem natural," Em murmured sleepily.

"How can we buy groceries when there's nobody in the town to sell them?" Oralee asked.

Em reached for the car door.

"You just wait," Mama told her. "You can't break into a store. We have to think of something."

Rosebud woke, but nothing happened.

Then I heard the *thwackety-thwackety-thwackety* of a helicopter. A minute later we were caught in its running lights.

"Mama!" My head felt hot and my hands felt cold. "What if . . . what if they got away from Sir Basil?"

She turned the key in the ignition and floored the accelerator. The engine strained and coughed and died.

"Run . . ." I fumbled for the door handle.

"With Oralee? With Em's blisters?" Mama turned the key again, but the engine didn't even groan.

The helicopter landed in the town square. The blades stopped. A dark figure descended from the machine and strode toward us.

Suddenly my brother sniffed the air. His furry ears twitched. Before I could stop him he scrambled from the car and shambled toward the figure. "Sir Basil!"

Mama turned off the ignition and let her breath

141

out slowly. Then she lifted Oralee out of the car. Em and I followed.

"Do we just call him Sir Basil? He won't expect me to curtsy or anything, will he?" Em whispered.

Chives stepped into the light.

"That," Em muttered, "is one tacky-looking nobleman."

"Where are EVIL and Beckwids?" I asked Sir Basil.

"I delivered them to a county jail. They'll be secure there until I return."

"We're starving," Rosebud told him. "I spilled all our soup."

"Shall we pop into the market then?" Chives walked to the door of the grocery store. "Confiscated all EVIL's keys. Most convenient."

As we stepped inside, he said, "You might as well take everything. It would all go to waste. There's a large reward for the capture of EVIL and Beckwids. I'll be happy to advance your portion of it and turn it over to EVIL for your purchases. Should keep them in shaving cream and dental floss while they await trial." He took a can of mixed nuts and a package of crackers off a shelf. "I'll be at City Hall, should you need me."

While there were not many things on the shelves, it was clear that EVIL lived well. Besides cans of fruit and vegetables, soups and sauces, there were packages of wild rice and noodles and pancake mix, jars of pickles and olives and mushrooms, and a refrigerated section with gallons of ice cream, fruit juices, frozen berries, quiche and pizza and pound cake.

The first thing we did was make sandwiches, starting with French bread and onion rolls and adding anything we'd ever thought would be interesting.

"Don't waste anything," our mother cautioned. We didn't.

She wandered through the aisles, exclaiming, "Croutons! Paper towels! Ice! Bags and bags of ice!"

When Rosebud selected the bottom box of the cereal display, she glanced at the cartons scattered on the floor and said, "Take them all."

We took almost everything, carting out jars and cans and boxes.

It was almost dawn now, and Sir Basil emerged from City Hall with his arms full of papers and folders. He put them in the helicopter, then came across and locked the grocery doors. "See if there's anything you want from the chemist's."

"Chemist's?" My brother groped for my hand.

"He means drugstore," Mama said, as Sir Basil unlocked the next door down.

It wasn't the greatest drugstore in the world. There were no magazines and no soda fountain, and a lot of pain relievers, bunion pads, and elastic bandages. Em was delighted, though, with the shampoos and fancy toothpastes and hairbrushes.

My brother managed to spray himself in the face with room deodorizer, so Mama had to haul him over to the town square fountain in the cold morning light. When she returned, Sir Basil helped her figure out her maps while she dried Rosebud.

"I don't know how we're going to *get* there," she said.

"Take EVIL's car. I'll reimburse them from your reward money."

Oralee was uneasy. "What about our van?"

"Oralee, I am doing the best I can," Mama told her.

As Chives began loading the helicopter, I went after him. "You're going?"

He paused. "To tell you the truth, Agnes, it makes me uneasy to be around a five-year-old . . . being . . . who is a walking crisis."

"You won't need him to testify?"

With Oralee trailing behind him, my brother ambled toward us, licking a frozen fruit bar and holding Forbisher.

Sir Basil was grave. "I think we might be wiser simply to take his statement, and then decide whether to use it. The problem is that those who see him would find it hard to believe him."

Rosebud looked hurt. "Who wouldn't believe me?"

"It's not that they wouldn't believe what you say," Chives soothed him. "It's that they wouldn't believe what they see. And you would present something of a national security problem. I mean, you're apt to create a general panic. Then there's the problem of suitable housing. Given the depths of human prejudice, we'd be hard put to find a decent hotel or even neighborhood to accept you. I can't bear to think of someone's little brother locked up in a zoo, or even a museum."

Rosebud gazed down at him. "You're not going to just *leave* us?"

A chunk of fruit bar plopped off the stick onto Chives' boot.

"I must . . . turn in all this evidence. . . ." Sir Basil climbed into the helicopter, and from there he waved goodbye.

Rosebud waved until the craft was out of sight. Then he waved a little longer. Then he wiped a great glistening tear from his snout. "I keep thinking of our van, all those flowers and curlicues, just left there in the forest. And the bron . . . the bron . . . *him* back there in the lake. Aggie, why are people always leaving everybody or having everybody leave them?"

Thirteen

It was late afternoon when we arrived at the land we'd inherited.

"At least the cabin is sound," Em said as we stepped on the porch.

Rosebud's leg went through a rotted plank.

Silently, Em helped him pull free.

The inside of that cabin was more disheartening than our old apartment.

There was a rusty iron cot with a blanket on it, a black iron stove, a wobbly wood table, and two unpainted wood chairs. On one wall was a shelf with a kettle, a warped skillet, a dented tin cup and plate, a dishpan, a bar of soap that something had chewed, and a folded, ragged towel. Against another wall leaned a pick, a shovel, and a straw broom.

"We'll just pretend we're prospectors," Mama said.

One good thing about being a child is that the world starts over each morning, and you can believe that the bad things that have happened every day up to then won't happen again, that you'll be smart and brave and all the things you want to be —until you see your brother is still a beast.

For breakfast, we heated square waffles and covered them with blueberries, and drank orange juice and fresh milk. "We'll have to use all that ice cream and frozen food before the ice gives out," Mama said.

When we stepped out of the house, a couple of squirrels ran up a tree right in front of us.

I heard water running, not a leaky faucet or a broken toilet, but strong, rowdy, free water. We followed the sound, and there, hidden from the cabin by only a few yards of trees, was a creek. It was so clear you could see the rocks in the stream bed and the speckled fish lazing with the current.

"Somebody grab Harry, quick!" Em said.

I noticed he was barely taller than she, now. He even seemed less shaggy.

It was fun, at first, hauling water from the creek, cleaning out the cabin, lying around the stove in the evening and feeling the warmth from it right to our bones. Each day Harry looked more and more like a little boy again.

But Mama worked as if she were working. "Got to get this place fit to sell."

"Mama!" I protested. "It's *ours,* and it's beautiful!"

"What about school?" she asked.

"Who needs school?" Oralee countered.

"Anybody who wants to have any say in how this world is run. Besides, Harry is practically himself now."

There's no fun in fixing up your home with the idea of leaving it. My sisters and Harry and I moped around, working halfheartedly.

On a cool morning with a muttering of thunder somewhere far off, I heard a vehicle laboring along the track to our place.

I stood outside the cabin, ready to run.

The flowers and the arabesques were gaudy as ever and the motor sounded as crochety. It stopped, and the driver waved to me.

"Mama!" I called. "It's Sir Basil, with our van!"

As Sir Basil climbed out of the van, Harry came running.

Chives gazed at him. "That handsome lad couldn't be . . ."

I nodded. "Harry."

We had lunch by the creek. We never asked

about EVIL or Beckwids—they'd left that much fear in us.

"Sorry everything we have is from jars and cans and packages." Mama passed the cashew nuts to Sir Basil. "It's strange, the things you miss. I keep remembering all the fresh fruits and salads we used to have when I was earning a living."

"There must be a village somewhere beyond here. I brought your share of the reward money, enough to buy—"

Mama smiled. "It's going to be a while before I go looking for any town beyond where I've been."

"Still, there's much to be said for seclusion." Sir Basil sat with his back against a log, Harry perched above him. "This spot is almost impossible to find."

Mama looked around her. "No place to raise a family."

"But so wonderfully out-of-the-way."

"Oh, it's beautiful. It's serene," Mama agreed. "But you can't bring up your children so they have no relation to their world. And Oralee's going to need her teeth straightened. Me—I hate to think I'd never see another stalk of celery. No, lovely as all this is, it's not for us, not full-time. I'll have to sell it for whatever I can get."

Sir Basil leaned back against the log. "I have no family to speak of, and no great fondness for greens and melons and the like. I might be interested in a retreat like this."

"You?" Mama asked.

"Mmm." He nodded. "The idea of being isolated like this, quiet, away from everything quite transcends any interest I may have in . . . in fresh carrots and parsnips. Have you any idea what it's like to spend your life with public menaces, never knowing what they may do next?"

"Oh, yes," Em said.

"This last business with EVIL and the count was the final straw, really, trying to write my report, going through the whole trial without mentioning"—he glanced at my brother—"things better left unmentioned."

"Wow! What things?" Harry leaned forward, fascinated, and fell off the log into Chives' lunch.

Sir Basil was a generous man—or he was desperate to buy a hideaway where he might repair his nerves.

We left him EVIL's car and took our van.

He stood outside the cabin watching us drive away, and he smiled.

I had never seen Sir Basil smile before.

So, after all we'd been through, we headed back toward the city we'd left.

We never got there.

Fourteen

Two days after we left Sir Basil, our van began to fail.

We managed to chug into a little town, and then the motor heaved and stopped.

While the van was being repaired, we stayed at a motel, and ate at coffee shops, and Mama took us to buy new shoes and jeans.

It was a quiet town. Most of the houses were old, with huge front yards full of thick short grass and hollyhocks, a dog lying across the walkway or a cat dozing on the front steps. Now and then a grown-up would come out of a house with lemonade for the kids running through the sprinklers.

Afternoons, there was a line outside the movie house, but my sisters and Harry and I felt shy about going to a movie in a strange town.

Three doors down from the movie house was an ice cream parlor. It had round, glass-topped tables with chipped edges, white wrought-iron chairs with red seat cushions, racks of comic books against one wall and candy cases near the other.

The woman who made our sundaes was old and slow and sociable. She gave us extra maraschino cherries because we were strangers.

"I can't do it for everybody," she said. "When the show lets out, kids will fill this place, and I'd be out of maraschinos in no time. That's one thing I'll miss—all the kids coming in to tell me about the movie. But me feet aren't what they used to be, and I've been promising me friend Dorrie for twenty years that I'd sell out and take that cruise we've planned since high school."

After Mama finished her sundae, she went and talked to the woman some more.

It turned out the woman wanted to sell her house as well, and move to a Florida condominium.

The house was an old two-bedroom cottage on a street shaded by oak and poplar trees. The backyard was full of blackberry vines and strawberry plants and small thoughtful toads.

A week after we moved in, Harry fell out of the walnut tree and broke his collarbone.

A broken bone is a sure conversation-starter, just as owning the only ice cream parlor in town is a certain way to make friends. A person who knows what the next flavor-of-the-month will be never lacks for acquaintances. Besides reading all the new comic books before we slid them onto our display racks, we had cases of candy at our fingertips.

It was nothing like a big-city store, of course. Nobody even suggested my mother should have a gun.

The interesting thing was how well our customers behaved. Then I began to realize why.

Little boys, bigger boys, and especially teenage boys would order cones, one after another, from Em, while they blushed and dropped their money and struggled to get out something more brilliant than "Almond fudge in a cake cone, please."

Fifteen

On a Monday morning in October, we were all up early. Mama wanted to restock the magazines before the store opened, and Oralee hadn't finished a book report.

"I'm going to die," Oralee groaned.

"Don't be silly." Em was snappish because the waffles she'd made had stuck to the waffle iron. "Everybody has to give an oral report in class sooner or later. You'll get used to it."

"I can't. If I had just one more day to get ready, just one day . . . My eyes feel hot. I think I have to throw up."

"That won't work, Oralee." Mama went on checking inventory sheets. "Clear your place and go find your shoes."

I heard a low howling outside.

Harry put his dishes on the counter by the sink and went to brush his teeth.

Em peered out the window. "Mama, look at the storm blowing up!"

Mama was absorbed in her lists. "Harry, did you leave your bike in the front yard?"

A splatter of rain hit the window. Mama looked up. Putting down her pencil, she went to the parlor. "The storm is only on the kitchen side of the house. Em, turn on the radio and see what's happening." She walked back to the bathroom.

When your mother strides with long, fast, heavy steps, you stay clear. Em and I couldn't resist following, but we lingered in the hall.

"I'm not saying it couldn't be a freak storm." Mama didn't raise her voice, but I was glad I wasn't the one she was addressing. "I'm just saying, Harry, that a second freak storm just better not happen around here in my lifetime. You understand?"

"Yes, ma'am." I could tell by his voice and his face in the mirror that he was intimidated and impressed.

". . . Meteorologists are baffled," the announcer on the kitchen radio was saying. "With gale force winds and heavy precipitation reported only between West Maple and the Elmwood School, and extending for a block around the school itself, officials have canceled all classes. The bizarre and localized storm pattern, along with the sudden onset . . ."

"I'll have to take you all to work with me," Mama said. "I can't leave you home in a storm like this." She went to finish dressing.

Harry continued brushing his teeth. He brushed very carefully, and for once he got no toothpaste on his shirt. Forbisher sat on the side of the sink, his back against the mirror.

"That bear's smile," Em murmured, "is not what it used to be."

"Come on, Em. The poor old thing almost got his head twisted off at Eel Manor. His stuffing is probably all shifted." Once you start agreeing with Em, there's no telling where it will end.

I could see what she meant, though. Forbisher did seem to have a small and secret smile I hadn't noticed before.